"I'm Suggesting That You Go Ahead With The Wedding."

"What in the world are you talking about? I can't have a wedding without a groom."

"I know. So I'm volunteering."

With a disbelieving shake of her head, Maribeth said, "You can't be serious!"

Chris met her bewildered gaze with a level one of his own. He let her see what was in his eyes, what he was feeling, before he replied, "I'm very serious, Maribeth."

Marriage with Chris? Why, she'd never thought of him in that way. At least…not exactly. He made her nervous in a way she couldn't quite describ . What would it be like to be married to him? To live with him? To make love—

"I can't take advantage of you," she said slowly.

Chris couldn't help but be amused. "Sure you can. You have my permission to take advantage of me any time, starting right now…."

Daughters of Texas: The hardest-working women in the land, the O'Brien sisters—Megan, Mollie and Maribeth—are three brides waiting to lasso the hearts of their very own cowboys!

Dear Reader,

Can you believe that for the next three months we'll be celebrating the publication of the 1000th Silhouette Desire? That's quite a milestone! The festivities begin this month with six books by some of your longtime favorites and exciting new names in romance.

We'll continue into next month, May, with the actual publication of Book #1000—by Diana Palmer—and then we'll keep the fun going into June. There's just so much going on that I can't put it all into one letter. You'll just have to keep reading!

This month we have an absolutely terrific lineup, beginning with *Saddle Up*, a MAN OF THE MONTH by Mary Lynn Baxter. There's also *The Groom, I Presume?*— the latest in Annette Broadrick's DAUGHTERS OF TEXAS miniseries. *Father of the Brat* launches the new FROM HERE TO PATERNITY miniseries by Elizabeth Bevarly, and *Forgotten Vows* by Modean Moon is the first of three books about what happens on THE WEDDING NIGHT. Lass Small brings us her very own delightful sense of humor in *A Stranger in Texas*. And our DEBUT AUTHOR this month is Anne Eames with *Two Weddings and a Bride*.

And next month, as promised, Book #1000, a MAN OF THE MONTH, *Man of Ice* by Diana Palmer!

Lucia Macro,
Senior Editor

Please address questions and book requests to:
Silhouette Reader Service
U.S.: 3010 Walden Ave., P.O. Box 1325, Buffalo, NY 14269
Canadian: P.O. Box 609, Fort Erie, Ont. L2A 5X3

Annette Broadrick

THE GROOM, I PRESUME?

SILHOUETTE *Desire*
Published by Silhouette Books
America's Publisher of Contemporary Romance

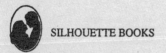

SILHOUETTE BOOKS

ISBN 0-373-05992-2

THE GROOM, I PRESUME?

Copyright © 1996 by Annette Broadrick

Printed in U.S.A.

Books by Annette Broadrick

Silhouette Desire

Hunter's Prey #185
Bachelor Father #219
Hawk's Flight #242
Deceptions #272
Choices #283
Heat of the Night #314
Made in Heaven #336
Return to Yesterday #360
Adam's Story #367
Momentary Marriage #414
With All My Heart #433
A Touch of Spring #464
Irresistible #499
A Loving Spirit #552
Candlelight For Two #577
Lone Wolf #666
Where There Is Love #714
*Love Texas Style! #734
*Courtship Texas Style! #739
*Marriage Texas Style! #745
Zeke #793
*Temptation Texas Style! #883
Mysterious Mountain Man #925
†Megan's Marriage #979
†The Groom, I Presume? #992

*Sons of Texas
†Daughters of Texas

Silhouette Romance

Circumstantial Evidence #329
Provocative Peril #359
Sound of Summer #412
Unheavenly Angel #442
Strange Enchantment #501
Mystery Lover #533
That's What Friends Are For #544
Come Be My Love #609
A Love Remembered #676
Married?! #742
The Gemini Man #796
Daddy's Angel #976
Impromptu Bride #1018
†Instant Mommy #1139

Silhouette Special Edition

Mystery Wife #877

Silhouette Books

Silhouette Christmas Stories 1988
"Christmas Magic"

Spring Fancy 1993
"Surprise, Surprise!"

Summer Sizzlers 1994
"Deep Cover"

ANNETTE BROADRICK

believes in romance and the magic of life. Since 1984, when her first book was published. Annette has shared her view of life and love with readers all over the world. In addition to being nominated by *Romantic Times* as one of the Best New Authors of that year, she has also won the *Romantic Times* Reviewers' Choice Award for Best in its Series for *Heat of the Night, Mystery Lover* and *Irresistible;* the Romantic Times WISH award for her heroes in *Strange Enchantment, Marriage Texas Style!* and *Impromptu Bride;* and the *Romantic Times* Lifetime Achievement Awards for Series Romance and Series Romantic Fantasy.

Dear Reader,

What an exciting time to be writing for the Silhouette Desire line. I'm pleased to be a part of the **Celebration 1000**. My first Desire was number 185, so I feel that I've been a part of the line for a long time.

Many things have changed in the world over the years since I began writing, but one thing has stayed the same—the need for warm, uplifting stories to remind us of the strength of the human spirit to overcome all obstacles and seek its fulfillment.

As long as we continue to want to share our hopes and dreams with others, Silhouette Books will be there with our stories.

Let the celebration continue.

Annette Broadrick

One

Chris Cochran slowed his late-model sports car and turned into the lane leading to the O'Brien ranch. He hadn't visited the ranch since he and Maribeth O'Brien had graduated from Texas A & M College. That had been four years ago.

Four years could be a long time in a person's life.

Seeing the ranch triggered all kinds of memories for him. In many ways, he was revisiting his childhood...the happiest times of his childhood.

Four years. He wondered what kind of changes had taken place in Maribeth's life in that time.

The ranch certainly looked prosperous these days. He wasn't surprised. Travis Kane, married to Maribeth's oldest sister, Megan, had built a fine reputation as a horse breeder and trainer since retiring from following the rodeo circuit.

As Chris followed the lane to the ranch headquarters located on a rise of one of the hills, he noted several new outbuildings had been erected on the place. In addition, there were new pastures fenced and neatly whitewashed. The lane, previously graveled, was now blacktopped.

The place looked good. Chris was pleased to know that the O'Brien family was doing all right.

Actually, Maribeth was the last member of the family still using the O'Brien name. When Megan had married Travis, there had been some talk around the county that the family might change the name of the ranch. That kind of talk was quickly stopped when the O'Brien sisters had reminded their friends and neighbors that the property had been known by that name for more than a hundred years. As long as any member of the original family continued to live there, the place would be known as the O'Brien ranch.

Chris pulled up and parked in front of the fence that separated the sprawling, native-stone-covered house from the rest of the buildings. He unfolded his long, rangy body and stretched. He'd left Dallas about five hours ago. Not too bad a driving time between the city and the hill country of central Texas.

"Well, look who's here!"

Chris smiled at the woman loping across the shaded lawn of the backyard toward him. "Chris Cochran, I almost didn't recognize you, it's been so long since you showed your face around here!" She opened the gate and waved him through. "City life must agree with you, cowboy. You're looking real good these days."

"It's good to see you, Megan," he said, giving her a quick hug. If she thought he was looking good, he could say the same about her with complete honesty. Married life definitely agreed with her.

He'd always liked Maribeth's sisters. They were loving, unpretentious people who made him feel accepted for himself. In the circles he now inhabited, he was cynically aware that the type of gushing attention he generally received was because he was Kenneth Cochran's sole heir.

"You remember Mollie, don't you?" Megan asked, motioning toward the other woman who now approached them. "We've been enjoying all this nice sunshine—after all those storms we've been having lately—by sitting outside and letting the kids play together. With the size of our families, we could start our own day-care center with no problem at all."

Chris nodded to the other sister and adjusted his Stetson, pulling it low on his forehead so that it rested just above his sunshades. "H'lo, Mollie."

"I take it you came down a few days early to visit with your mom and grandparents before the wedding, huh?" Megan asked, grinning. "You ready to get all duded up for everybody to stare at?"

"I imagine I'll be able to muddle through all right," he drawled. "Speaking of the wedding, is Maribeth around?" He glanced around the area, not seeing her with the children who were still playing well together, despite their mothers' momentary lack of attention.

"Of course she is," Megan replied. "Since we finished the new barn for the horses, she practically sleeps out there, looking after the new arrivals. Maybe you'll have better luck getting her out of there than we have. You can tell her we've got fresh lemonade up here for both of you."

Chris looked back at the newest and largest building on the property, before returning his gaze to Megan. "I'll see what I can do, but I'm not promising anything. Maribeth is a law unto herself.''

"Don't I know it," Megan agreed.

She *should* know, Chris thought as he crossed the ranch yard to the building that sprawled across the way. Megan had been both mother and father to Maribeth since their parents had been killed. Megan had been barely sixteen at the time, while Mollie had been ten years old and Maribeth eight.

He felt nothing but admiration for that kind of family love and loyalty, neither of which had been part of his childhood. Perhaps that was why he'd sometimes envied Maribeth when they'd been children together.

She took for granted all the love and mutual respect that surrounded the three sisters and their families. He, on the other hand, considered the many warm relationships something of a miracle. He could only witness their interactions with a certain amount of awe.

Chris studied the horse barn as he approached it, amazed at how well the structure had been designed. Stalls ran the length of the barn on either side of a wide walkway. Each stall had two doorways—one that opened out into an enclosed pasture, while the other gave access from inside.

He heard Maribeth before he saw her. She was softly crooning, no doubt getting one of the newborns used to the touch and presence of a human being.

Chris's pulse automatically picked up in anticipation, even before she came into view. He was amused by his reaction, but not surprised by it. He'd had the same reaction around her ever since they were kids. Some things just never changed.

He paused at the gate to the stall where she was grooming a colt, her voice a steady stream of honeyed endearments while she gently stroked the animal with both hands, only one of which held a currycomb. Since she was unaware of his presence, Chris took the rare moment to study the woman he'd been in love with since he'd first seen her when they were in the third grade.

She'd always reminded him of a shooting star—a blazing flash of light across a darkened sky—once seen, never forgotten. As a child, she'd been filled with vitality and exuberance, eager to embrace the world. The years had subdued very little of that spark, thank God.

The bright red hair of early childhood had darkened gradually over the years, but it maintained its vibrant shade, no doubt still causing heads to turn for a second glance.

Not that Maribeth ever noticed.

One of her most endearing qualities was her blindness to her own beauty. She was totally unconscious of the fact that her tall slender figure, her fair, creamy skin and her wide-set golden eyes could have easily graced the covers of innumerable magazines around the world.

She'd always been oblivious to her looks. Instead she'd grown up wearing boots and jeans, a typical tomboy who enjoyed ranching life and gave very little thought to the world outside of Agua Verde.

Maribeth had been aware of only one male since Chris had known her—Bobby Metcalf. She'd always been Bobby's shadow, while growing up. And Bobby Metcalf had been Chris's closest friend from grade school through college.

So Chris had contented himself with being a part of a small group of friends who spent their time together, never letting on to anyone how he truly felt about Maribeth.

He'd just been grateful for both of their friendships. Without them, his childhood would have been very lonely.

Bobby had given Maribeth an engagement ring for Christmas their senior year in college. Not that anyone who knew them had been surprised. They'd been talking about getting married someday as far back as high school, but for some reason, the ring made everything more real to Chris, symbolizing all that he would never be able to share with her.

Once the three of them had graduated from college, Chris had deliberately stayed away from Agua Verde. He'd recognized that the time had come for him to make a clean break and to get on with his life.

No doubt Maribeth had made the right choice for her. He couldn't really say that his heart had been broken. How could it be? They had never been more than friends. She'd never given him any reason to suggest that she saw him as anyone other than Bobby's best friend.

No. His heart wasn't broken. Maybe dented a little, but there had never been any doubt in his mind that he would recover.

Bobby should be here now, not me, Chris thought with more than a little frustration. He'd lost track of the many times in their lives when he'd wanted to wring Bobby's neck, but never had he felt the urge more strongly than today.

"Hello, Maribeth," he finally said to the woman he'd come to see. He kept his voice low in order not to startle either the woman or the colt.

At the sound of the familiar deep voice Maribeth froze. She hadn't heard it in years, but once heard, Chris Cochran's voice could never be forgotten.

She spun around and saw him standing in the shadows of the barn. For a moment she forgot to breathe. What in the world was the matter with her? This was Bobby's friend, Chris.

He looked different, somehow, standing there watching her impassively. His youthful good looks had matured into a formidably handsome, mysterious man. She recalled that nobody had been able to figure out what Chris was thinking. He made a great poker player for that reason.

A tiny shiver danced along her spine. He'd always affected her that way. She wasn't certain why. There was just an air about him, an aloofness that had always made her feel the slightest twinge of nervousness whenever he was around. And yet...there was no one in her life whom she trusted more.

"Chris," she whispered, almost to herself, while she slipped through the gate to where he stood. She paused, gripping the currycomb tighter. "You're early!" Then she felt really stupid to have blurted out such a statement. "I mean, you must be here to visit your mother and grandparents. It's good to see you."

His dark eyes always seemed to look deep into her soul. She felt as though any secrets she might have would be easy for him to read.

"Looks like life's been treating you fair enough," he said, deliberately covering his intense reaction to her. "You look as frisky as one of those fillies out there." He motioned to one of the enclosed pastures with a nod of his head.

She chuckled nervously, and used the back of her wrist to shove wisps of curls off her forehead. "I look like a saddle tramp, and I know it. As you can see, I wasn't expecting company." She looked around as though unsure of what to do next. "I, uh, didn't expect to see you for another couple of days. I suppose Bobby told you the wedding rehearsal and dinner are scheduled for Friday." She turned away and began to straighten various items hanging on the side of the stall.

"Yeah, he told me." He glanced around the barn. "Looks like you've got enough to keep you busy these days."

She picked up a saddle blanket and motioned him to follow her back to the tack room. "Well, I needed to do something. Once Bobby decided to follow in Travis's footsteps and take up the rodeo circuit, Travis offered to give me a job as one of the trainers."

"He's doing well, isn't he?"

"Travis? You bet. Things couldn't be better."

"I was thinking about Bobby."

She continued to be too busy to look at him. "Yes. He's making a real name for himself."

Maribeth put the currycomb and saddle blanket away before leading the way to the entrance of the barn. Pausing in the wide doorway, she looked out at the view.

"You know, Chris, sometimes it's hard for me to realize that the three of us are twenty-six years old. You and Bobby left and started working on your careers, while I seem to have gotten caught up in some kind of time warp." She turned and faced him, wrapping her arms around her waist. "All I've done is stay here on the ranch. I've spent most of my life here." She gave her head a tiny shake. "Not that I'm complaining. Bobby and I always planned to live on his family's place after we got married. It's the only life I know, after all. It just seems a little strange to realize that four years have gone by and I've done nothing more with my life."

"When was the last time you talked to Bobby?"

She tilted her head back and closed her eyes. "Let me think. He called last week. He was in Nashville at the time. He'd done well and was high on his success. However, he made a cross-his-heart-and-hope-to-die promise that he would be here no later than noon on Friday." She looked at him as though daring him to doubt Bobby's word.

Chris nodded, unwilling to comment on that particular subject at the moment. "He's still winning a goodly share of the bull-riding events, I suppose."

"Yep, trying his best to win world champion. You know that's been his dream for years." She grinned at Chris. "I doubt that he'll ever beat Travis's record, but he sure wants to try. He deserves that chance."

Chris had his own opinion of what Bobby deserved, but once again, he refrained from sharing it with her. Instead he motioned to the new pastures and their occupants with a sweeping arm gesture. "Speaking of Travis, this is quite an operation he's got going here. I'm impressed."

"Isn't it amazing? He's really done well. Of course he'd built a name for himself in the business while he was following the circuit, which didn't hurt when he decided to stay home. Every time I ask Bobby when he's going to head back home, he reminds me of the legend of Travis Kane and how much effort he needs to work in order to make as big a splash."

"I guess I've lost touch with what's been happening in Agua Verde county these past few years. I thought Bobby was already working with his dad until he called to ask me to be his best man at the wedding. I guess I'd sort of figured you'd gone ahead and gotten married without inviting me."

"You should know better than that, Chris. Bobby would never get married without you by his side. Y'all used to talk about that. You'd each be there for the other."

"I remember. I'll admit I was surprised to find out he'd been traveling for most of these years. It must have been hard on you."

Maribeth heard the sympathy in his voice. Darn it. Seeing Chris again so unexpectedly was bringing up all kinds of emotions that she wasn't ready to deal with. But wasn't that normal for a bride-to-be? She wasn't having any doubts. Of course not. Why, she'd loved Bobby forever and then some. In three days she would be married, after years of making plans.

"I'll admit that I've missed him during some of his longer road trips. At first, he'd come home every week or two. Then later, it was mostly a month at a time before he'd make it home." She could no longer hold Chris's steady gaze and looked away. "It will be different once we're married."

"Will it?"

She glanced back at him. "Well, of course it will. We'll be living together, then. He'll be home more."

"Has he told you that? Or is that what you're hoping?"

"Well, if he's still traveling, then I'll go with him." She tilted her chin slightly. "There won't be anything wrong with his wife traveling with him. He just needs a little time to settle down, that's all. He's still young."

Chris raised one of his eyebrows quizzically. "We're all the same age, remember?"

Maribeth smiled. "Maybe so, but you were born old, Chris. I swear. When I look back at some of the things the three of us did together when we were kids, I figure the only way we managed to scrape by as well as we did was because you always saved our butts.''

"Well, you have to admit that you and Bobby are a bit impulsive.''

She shook her head emphatically. "Not me. Not anymore. I'm grown up now." She waved to the row of stalls behind them. "I'm steadily employed, thanks to Travis. I have a fulfilling job, a great family and a whole passel of nieces and nephews. Why, my life couldn't be better!''

What could he possibly say to that? He let the silence that fell between them speak for itself. When it stretched into an uncomfortable length, Chris reached over and gently tugged on the thick plait of hair draped over her shoulder. "How about taking a ride with me?" he asked. "I'll show off my newest toy.''

He could almost see the tension leaving her body. She pushed the wisps of hair off her forehead with a gesture that made him ache with a sense of tenderness.

"Sounds great," she said. "Let's go.''

"You won't get in trouble for sneaking away from work, will you?" His tone was teasing and she responded with a lighthearted chuckle.

"Are you kidding? Travis is always complaining that I spend too many hours out here, and that by comparison I make him look like a lazy bum.''

They strolled toward his car. "I'm amazed at the number of changes that have been made to this place since I was last here.''

She gave his arm a gentle tap with her fist. "All that shows is that you haven't been visiting often enough. I figured that once you'd moved to Big D, you didn't have time for us country yokels.''

"That's not true. I've just been really busy.''

"Doing what? You used to talk about working for your father after graduation. Is that what you're doing?"

"In a sense. I pilot one of the company planes whenever they're shorthanded. I guess you would call me a troubleshooter. I fill in wherever I'm needed."

Maribeth stopped in her tracks. "You're a pilot? I never knew that!"

"Yeah. I started taking lessons as a teenager while I spent my summers in Dallas with my dad."

"You never said a word about it."

"It wasn't something to be tossed into a conversation."

"But it was something you were interested in, something obviously important to you. I remember you would listen to me when I was going on about all my pet projects whenever we got back together after summer vacations. But you never said a word."

"It was no big deal, Maribeth. Really."

She just shook her head. "Sometimes I think you work at being a mystery man."

"What are you talking about?"

"You know. I remember in school how all the girls acted around you. You'd come back each year with this big-city polish, rarely talking to anyone, and never about yourself. It used to drive us crazy."

He laughed. "Well. Now you know one of my deep, dark secrets. I was spending summer vacations playing up in the clouds. Feel better now?"

They had paused by his tomato red sports car. He leaned past her and opened the passenger door. She got a whiff of after-shave that brought back even stronger memories of the young man she used to know. She'd always liked that particular scent. When she'd asked him about it once, he said it was a gift from his father one year and he'd used it ever since. It smelled expensive, woodsy, and infinitely male.

She searched frantically for something casual to say. "I'm a little surprised that you're content to stay in a large city after spending so many years living here on a ranch."

"That was more my mother's choice. She never liked living in the city."

She tapped his large, silver belt buckle. "You still dress like a country boy, what with that hat, fancy buckle and boots. What is it they say? 'You can take the boy out of the country, but...'"

"I suppose I'll always be a country boy at heart, but I don't think I could ever make ranching my life. I need a challenge that I can come to grips with... not worrying over the price of beef and the uncertainties of the weather." He motioned for her to get into the car.

She paused, and waved to the two women who were watching them from comfortably reclined lawn chairs.

"Megan, if Travis comes looking for me, tell him I'll be back in a little while." With a wink toward him, she added, "Chris is going to take me for a ride in his fancy little car."

"Are you going to take that from her?" Megan asked without moving. "She doesn't deserve such courtesy if she's going to make fun of your trusty steed."

Chris walked around the car, saying, "The woman has no taste. We all know that, now, don't we?"

They pulled away amid the laughter of the three women. Ever curious, Maribeth scrutinized the dash, peeked behind the seats at the area that was little more than a shelf, then settled back into the luxurious leather seats with a sigh.

"I should have been watching you closer. How in the world did you manage to get into this thing? With a shoehorn?"

"It's not so bad once you get used to it." He pointed to the floor. "At least there's plenty of legroom once you're inside."

She just shook her head. "It'll never take the place of a full-size pickup truck." She glanced around her once again. "Why, you could barely haul anything in this dinky li'l ol' thing."

Chris tried to stifle his laugh, then gave up, allowing the laughter to ease the tension he was feeling. "Maribeth, you are definitely one of a kind."

She looked at him in surprise. "What's that supposed to mean?"

"Just that. You're definitely unique."

"Is there anything wrong with that?"

"Not at all. There are times when I find myself envying your attitude toward life. You're content with what you have. I've never known you to yearn for something someone else has."

She grinned. "That's because I already have everything I want."

After a pause, he said in a more sober voice. "Everything?"

She glanced at him in surprise. "What more could I possibly want? I have my family, and in three days I'm marrying the man I've loved most of my life. As the old saying goes—'who could ask for anything more?'"

"I know you must have had a tough adjustment, coming back to Agua Verde while Bobby took off to follow his dream. That took a lot of courage for you, not objecting to his plans when you expected to get married as soon as we graduated."

"I was really naive back then, wasn't I? Just because I was ready to get married didn't mean that Bobby felt the same way. I guess that's the biggest difference between men and women. Men want to take longer to find themselves or whatever." She looked out the window, then back at Chris. "I probably wouldn't admit this to another soul, but when Bobby first left, I thought I would die from missing him, missing all the fun times the three of us used to have together."

"I know what you mean. It felt really strange to live in Dallas year-round."

She looked at him, surprised. "You missed us? I find that hard to imagine. You always seemed to be content with your own company... sort of a loner, you know?"

"Yeah. I know."

They rode along in silence for a while before Maribeth began to speak, her voice very soft. "For those first few months after he left, I would lie in bed at night, thinking about him being so far away. Wondering if he missed me as much as I missed him. Then I thought about how it would have been if we had gotten married, and he'd gone on the road afterward. Finally I consoled myself with the fact that at least we'd never been—" She paused and cleared her throat. "Uh, we'd never had—been intimate." Talking faster, she said, "I think that would have made it so much worse, knowing what I was missing while he was away. It was bad enough just imagining what it might have been like to..." After a longer pause, she muttered, "Oh, you know what I'm trying to say."

Chris turned off the highway they'd been on and followed a little-used road until it ended at the top of bluffs overlooking one of the rivers in the county.

"Why don't we get out here and enjoy the view while we talk, okay?" He reached behind his seat and grabbed a blanket.

"Sure. Why not?" Maribeth hopped out of the car and looked around. "I haven't been here in years. We used to come here when we were kids, remember?"

"Oh, yes. I remember everything we ever did together."

He spread the blanket on the ground and they sat side by side, looking across the Texas hills to the horizon.

Chris waited to see if Maribeth was going to say anything more. When she didn't, he cleared his throat, then gruffly said, "I know it's none of my business, but I'd just assumed that you and Bobby had already been intimate. I mean, neither one of you has ever dated anyone else, through high school or college. I just figured that kind of commitment was because— Well, you know what I'm saying. I guess that's why I've been so surprised that he could stay on the road for so long, all the time knowing that you were here, waiting for him."

He gave her a quick, sideways glance in time to see her face turn as rosy as her hair.

"Um, well, I guess lots of people have assumed that." She turned so that she was facing him. "I'm not sure that anybody else but you could possibly understand this, Chris—" she began, then stopped.

Chris swallowed. Well, hell. He'd brought up the subject, hadn't he? And it looked as though she was going to unburden herself. He just wasn't certain he was ready to hear all that she was going to say.

He was still reeling from the sudden knowledge that she had never made love to his childhood buddy. That news went a long way toward helping him forgive Bobby for his thoughtless behavior.

She leaned back on her elbows, still looking off into the distance. "You remember how it was when we were growing up. Bobby and I never really paired off. We were always with the group, or at least with you."

Chris thought about that before drawling, "You never seemed to mind."

Her eyes quickly met his and she shifted, as though slightly restless. "Oh, I wasn't trying to imply that you were in the way. It was just the way things were for us. You remember."

He nodded, allowing himself to relax a little.

"It seems strange talking to anyone about it. I mean, really, there's nobody that I could have talked to about it, even back then. Maybe there was something a little weird about us. I know of other couples in high school who were quite open about their relationships, and there were several. But Bobby and me—I don't know. We just didn't fool around. Of course we did our share of parking and necking, but for me at least, I was a little afraid of the whole idea of it. I mean, who could I talk to about it, anyway? Can you imagine what Megan would have said or done if I'd asked her any questions about it? Besides, Travis and Deke would have used Bobby for coyote bait if they'd thought he was fooling around with me when we were in school! Just the thought of accidentally getting pregnant would freeze my blood. There was no way I could have faced Megan with that kind of news."

She gave him a quick glance from beneath her lashes and chuckled. "I guess I was lucky that Bobby never really pushed the limits I set. I'm not sure why, exactly. We never really talked about it." She sat cross-legged, her elbows resting on her knees.

"Looking back to that time, what I remember was how much fun we had together, the whole group of us. Remember how it was? We were always going places, doing things, having fun with the gang." She seemed to be thinking out loud, as she said, "Growing up the way we did on a ranch, it wasn't as if we didn't know what's supposed to happen and all, but still— Knowing about it isn't the same as actually doing it, is it?"

Her face glowed with embarrassment but she kept her gaze steady as she faced him.

"I think you were very wise, myself," he said with a great deal of sincerity.

Maribeth felt a wave of an unidentified emotion sweep over her at his words, as though she'd been seeking his approval, which was ridiculous. What was the matter with her today, anyway? Although Chris had been a part of her life for years, she'd never been so open with him before. Hoping to turn the tables, she suddenly demanded, "What about you?"

"Me!" He almost strangled spitting the word out. "What about me?"

Good. She'd managed to get past his guard that time. "You know exactly what I'm talking about. If I'm going to be confessing all about my nonexistent sex life on the eve of my wedding, I figure you owe me a tale or two in return, just so I won't feel alone."

He eyed her warily. "Such as?"

"Such as filling me in on some of your activities while we were at A & M. I remember you dated several classmates during that time."

He cleared his throat and then smiled. It was the sexiest, most seductive smile Maribeth had ever witnessed. Her heart began to pound in her chest. Darn, but this man had a lethal charm that she was much too inexperienced to know how to handle. "My mama always told me that a gentleman keeps his mouth shut," he finally drawled.

She fought to control her responses. Working to sound as unaffected as she knew how, Maribeth murmured, "Mmm-hmm. And you're always a gentleman, right?"

"I try my damnedest, ma'am. I most sincerely do."

They laughed together, effectively breaking the tension that had suddenly sprung up between them.

Maribeth impulsively reached over and touched his hand, then jerked back as though she'd accidentally touched a hot coal. "I'm glad you came to see me today. I've missed having you as part of my life."

He deliberately took her hand and held it firmly in his. "I've missed you, too."

The tension immediately surrounded them once again.

Maribeth nervously began to talk. "You know, being the youngest sister hasn't always been the easiest thing for me, especially as I've gotten older. Do you realize that both Megan and Mollie were married and had children by the time they reached my age?"

Her palm was tingling where it was pressed against his. She looked down at his darkly tanned hand. It was strong, engulfing hers. She forced herself to look into his dark eyes. There was a warmth there that made her feel accepted.

Impulsively she asked, "Have you ever wanted a brother or sister in your life, Chris?"

She could almost see his withdrawal although his body hadn't moved in the slightest. "Not really. Being an only child was complicated enough, given my family history. Although, looking back, it might have been nice to have someone else there."

"As much as I fuss about Megan always playing mother-hen with me, I'm really grateful to have her in my life. Mollie, too. It's strange to think about it. Mollie's only two years older than me, and she's already been married eight years and has three children. Wow. It's hard to realize time has gone by so quickly."

"She seems happy enough."

"Oh, yeah. Deke's obviously crazy about her and it's easy to see how she feels about him." For a moment she was caught up in her memories. "I wouldn't have dreamed when I watched them get married that I would still be single so many years later."

Chris watched her through his lashes. Damn, but it was good to see her, to be with her again! He'd pushed his feelings for her away for so long that he'd almost convinced himself that they were no longer there . . . or real. This time with her had quickly disabused him of that notion.

They'd been out there on the bluffs for almost an hour and he still hadn't told her what he needed to tell her. Dear God, but he hated this.

She was staring out over the river to the surrounding hills, looking relaxed enough. He still held her hand in his. She might look relaxed, but there was a slight tremor in her fingers.

"Maribeth?"

She slowly turned her head toward him. "Hmm?"

"Bobby called me last night." His voice sounded harsh to his ears.

He felt her hand stiffen in his. She tugged, silently requesting release, which he reluctantly gave her.

She watched him warily, and he knew that on some level she had been expecting something like this. Regardless, it didn't make his job any easier.

"He was in Las Vegas."

She had been bracing herself for something, even though she wasn't certain what it was. All kinds of thoughts had dashed around in her head. He was hurt. He was going to postpone the wedding, he was— What? Why would he have called Chris and not her? Why—?

"Las Vegas? What in the world is he doing there? He said he'd be in Oklahoma this week and would be through there by tomorrow."

"He asked me to come down here to see you."

She fought to hang on to her composure. "Why? What is it, Chris? Just tell me."

He reached for her hands, already feeling the coldness that had washed through her. "He wanted me here because he didn't want you to be alone when you heard his news."

"What?" she whispered.

"Bobby got married last night."

TWO

She stared at him blankly for a long moment without blinking. When the silence seemed as if it would stretch into infinity she silently mouthed the word "married?" as though it was a foreign word she'd never heard.

Chris waited, knowing there was nothing else he could say. There was no way to make this easy for her. He could almost see the pain as it seemed to inch its way into her consciousness.

As though finally remembering to breathe, she took a quick breath, then released it. Another moment passed, another gasp of air followed, as though she had to remind herself of her lungs' continual need for life-sustaining oxygen.

"I don't understand," she finally said. Her mouth quivered, then was still. As though searching for words that might make some sense to her, she asked, "Why would Bobby call you and say such a thing? Bobby would never..."

What little breath she had, suddenly deserted her. She paused, her hand pressed against her throat, her eyes mutely pleading for him to tell her that this was all a joke.

Chris could feel her pain just as surely as if it was his. In many ways, it was. He would have done anything in his power not to hurt this woman.

"Chris, surely he was teasing. Surely he didn't really mean that he—" Her breath was coming in short pants, as though she'd been running hard.

"He said that a bunch of the group had been out celebrating, partying. He admitted that he didn't remember too much about the night. Vegas was mentioned, it was like a joke or something. He couldn't fill in details and I didn't ask for any. When he woke up the next day he realized what he had done. He knew he had to let you know. He found that he couldn't call you and just tell you like that. So he called me, instead."

She looked at Chris with dawning awareness. "All this time you've been here... we've been talking about the past, and the wedding..." Her voice trailed off. She spoke as if to herself. "I was even discussing my sex life with you, for Pete's sake." Her eyes suddenly filled with tears and Chris felt as though he'd been punched in the gut. "All this time you knew that Bobby had— That Bobby—"

Suddenly she jerked away from him, jumping to her feet. "I don't believe you," she said in a hoarse voice, her back to him. "Why, the whole idea is absurd. The invitations have all gone out, everything's been planned for months... for years! Bobby wouldn't suddenly do something so—" Her voice broke. Without looking at him, she walked back to the car. In a low voice, she said, "I'd like to go home now."

Chris reluctantly followed her. "I don't think that's a good idea right at the moment, do you?" he asked reasonably. "That's why I brought you out here. So you could have some time alone, to get used to the idea."

The look she gave him was chilling. "Get *used* to the idea? How, exactly, do you propose I do that? Am I supposed to calmly dismiss and forget the past fifteen years of my life?"

"No. Of course not. Damn it, Maribeth. I know I didn't do this right, but how the hell do you tell a person something like this? You had to know. He sure as hell left it a little late to pull a stunt like this, then leave it for me to tell you. I came as soon as I could."

"Fine." Once again she turned away, this time opening the door to the car and getting inside. "You've told me. Thank you very much. Now I'd like to go home."

She'd left the door open. Chris took advantage of that by hunkering down beside her. Taking her hand, he said, "Don't shut me out, honey, okay? I know you're hurt by this. But I'm here for you. You've got me. Does that help?"

Gentleness from this particular man was more than she could handle. The tears she'd desperately been fighting to contain finally spilled over and rolled down her cheeks. She could do nothing to stop them.

Awkwardly he pulled her into his arms. The sudden reminder of his after-shave teased her senses, whisking her away to a younger, more innocent time.

"I don't want to cry," she said fiercely into his shoulder, ineffectually wiping her eyes.

"You're entitled," he murmured. He fumbled in his back pocket and brought out a crisp, neatly folded handkerchief, silently offering it to her.

She straightened, taking the handkerchief and energetically wiping her eyes and cheeks. "How could he do something like this?" Her voice broke and she jammed her fist against her mouth to muffle a sob. She waited until she could gain some control before saying, "It's like a nightmare, a scary dream brought on by prewedding jitters. It's like some kind of a test. What would you do if you planned a wedding and your fiancé didn't show up? It's a giant, cosmic joke. Isn't the bride being left at the altar a cliché?"

"Look, why don't we go back over there and sit for a while? I know I'd be more comfortable," he added lightly, glancing down at his awkward position beside the small car. "Maybe we can work out some kind of plan."

Maribeth glanced at Chris and tried to smile. She wasn't certain how successful her attempt was, but she reminded herself that she had to stop thinking of herself for a moment. Bobby had put both her and Chris into a horrible situation here. Why should she take her feelings out on Chris? He was only trying to help.

With a nod, she moved her legs to get out of the car. Chris immediately stood and offered her his hand. When she was standing beside him, he put his arms around her.

"I know you're hurt, but you and I both know that Bobby has never been a role model for responsibility. In a way, this is very typical of the kid I used to know. I had just assumed he'd grown up some...until that phone call last night."

Maribeth was furious that she couldn't stop crying. The tears slid down her cheeks quicker than she could wipe them away. This was so stupid, getting upset this way. It certainly didn't solve anything.

She leaned against Chris, grateful for his warmth and for his understanding.

He turned and with one arm still around her shoulders, guided her back to the blanket. He helped her to sit, then lowered himself beside her.

They sat there in silence. Maribeth lost track of the time. So many thoughts raced through her mind, none of them making much sense. Chris was no longer touching her, but she knew he was there.

Eventually she asked, "Did he say who it was?"

For a moment, she thought he wasn't going to answer. When he did, his voice was low. "No. I didn't ask. That wasn't the purpose of his call."

"I suppose." After another lengthy pause, she said, "It's probably somebody who follows the circuit. She's probably been there for him whenever he needed consoling or cheering. She's probably—"

"Don't, honey. Don't start to imagine stuff that you have no way of knowing if it's true or not. Trying to second-guess the situation doesn't do any good. It will only make you feel worse."

Her attempt at a laugh was a dismal failure. "Feel worse? Surely you're kidding."

Silence fell between them once more.

Eventually Chris said, "I know you don't believe this right at the moment, but I know that things are going to be okay for you eventually. It isn't the end of the world, even though it may feel like it. Someday, you'll be able to look back at all of this and see how God's plans for us aren't necessarily what we had in mind at the time. Maybe He has other plans we aren't aware of at the moment. Just give yourself some time to deal with what's happened, and I think you'll do fine."

There was nothing more he could think of to say. So he sat there beside her, staring out over the hills, and waited for her to deal with the news in her own way. He knew she was crying, but she never made a sound, other than her uneven breathing and an occasional sniff. She was handling it as well as anyone could. He'd never been more proud of her.

And now she's free, a small voice in his head reminded him.

So what?

So now's your chance.

Oh, sure.

Think about it. Maybe something can be salvaged from this mess Bobby has created. Just think about it.

The sun sank lower in the west, tinting the sky with wisps of pastel colors. He'd forgotten how beautiful the Texas hill country was. The gentle breeze cooled them, wafting the scent of cedar across the hills.

He had no idea how long they had been sitting in silence when she finally spoke once again.

"He was right."

"About what?"

"Not telling me over the phone."

"Yes. At least he did something right."

She sighed, her breath still catching. "I'm glad you were here, Chris." She gave him a quick glance before looking away. "It would have been even tougher if I'd been at home, with the family, trying to explain." She sighed. "I just feel overwhelmed at the moment. I don't know where to start."

Her voice sounded stronger. She was more in control of her emotions. He took the chance of resting his hand on her back. When she leaned into him slightly, he began to massage the area between her shoulder blades.

"Start what?"

"Telling everybody the wedding is canceled." The tears that had dried up earlier suddenly reappeared. She impatiently wiped them away, then blew her nose on the handkerchief. "I feel like such a dope, patiently waiting for years for him to return home to marry me when all this time he— He's been—"

There was no reason for her to finish that particular line of thought.

"You know what?" he said, making the effort to sound brisk and matter-of-fact. "What you really need to do is to get away from here for a while. Why don't you come back to Dallas with me? I've got a big place with plenty of room. It would give you a chance to distance yourself from the situation until you can come to terms with what's happened."

His suggestion brought a quiver to her lips, as though she was attempting to smile. "You've got to be kidding, Chris." Yes. Definitely a watery smile. "I'd never hear the end of it from my family if I went off somewhere with you."

"We could get around that."

Her expression when she cut her eyes around to look at him clearly showed her doubt.

"I have a suggestion that might solve some of this for you."

"What? Put a notice in the paper? I already thought of that, but it's too late. The weekly paper will be out in the morning."

"No. I'm suggesting that you go ahead with the wedding."

"What in the world are you talking about? I can't have a wedding without a groom."

"I know. So I'm volunteering."

She straightened away from him, pushing herself up until she was standing, looking down at him. With a disbelieving shake to her head, she said, "You can't be serious!"

Chris took his time getting up. When they were facing each other once again, he met her bewildered gaze with a level one of his own. He let her see what was in his eyes, what he was feeling, before he replied, "I'm very serious, Maribeth."

If she lived to be a hundred, Maribeth knew that she would never experience a day like this one. "Why?" Blurted out that way, her response had sounded almost insulting.

"I have many reasons, none of which matter in the least if you find the idea repulsive."

Marriage to Chris Cochran repulsive? Many feelings came to mind, but repulsion wasn't one of them. For a day filled with shocking disclosures, this one was as great as any she'd heard so far.

Marriage with Chris? Why, she'd never thought of him in that way. At least...not exactly. Even though she had teased him earlier today about the women in his life, he'd always seemed too much of a loner for her to ever imagine him married to anyone.

He made her nervous in a way she couldn't quite describe. What would it be like to be married to him? To live with him? To sleep with him? To make love—

Well! He'd certainly taken her mind off the news he'd brought. She'd gotten so caught up in his proposal—and that was exactly what it was, she realized with a dazed fascination—that she had momentarily forgotten that the entire county was going to turn out for her wedding in three days, unless she got busy and explained to everyone what had happened.

Chris wished he knew what she was thinking. Her expressive face revealed a bewildering series of thoughts and feelings, none of which he'd been able to decipher.

"This doesn't sound at all like you, Chris," she finally said. "You're not the impulsive type. So why would you suggest something so unusual?"

He took her hand, placed it on his palm and traced the length of her fingers with his other hand. "What's so unusual about it? Think about it for a moment. You've been planning to get married for sometime now. You can still get married. You've known me for almost as long as you've known Bobby, so it's not as if we're strangers. You pointed out earlier that you had spent most of your life on the ranch. Well, now you can come with me and see something more of the world."

"I can't take advantage of you," she said slowly, her gaze fixed on their linked hands.

Chris couldn't help but be amused. She sounded so earnest. And so scared. "Sure you can. You have my permission to take advantage of me at anytime, starting right now." He released her hands and tipped her chin up so that she could see his face. He'd never been more sincere in his life when he said, "I can't think of anything that would give me more pleasure than to marry you, Maribeth."

Her expression was difficult to make out. It was only then that he realized the light was fading rapidly from the sky.

"Oh, Chris," she said in the gathering darkness. He could hear the tears in her voice. She wiped her hand impatiently across her eyes once again. "I don't know what to say."

A surge of exultation shot through him. She hadn't turned him down cold. Was it fair to take advantage of her while she was so vulnerable?

Something needed to be done. And done quickly.

Giving in to temptation, Chris slid his arm around her waist and with his other hand, tilted her chin upward. Moving slowly in order to give her time to stop him if she wished, he leaned closer until his lips brushed hers.

She didn't flinch and she didn't pull away. That was enough encouragement for him to put all the yearning he felt into the kiss that he'd fantasized giving her for more years than he could remember.

Her lips were even softer than he had imagined. She tasted of tears and temptation. He took his time molding his mouth to fit hers, easing his way as her innocence imprinted itself on him.

He pressed her against him, his hands exploring her back from her nape to the base of her spine while he nudged her lips apart and dipped into the sweetness of her mouth.

By the time Maribeth understood that Chris intended to kiss her, he was already doing it. The first touch of his mouth froze her into immobility. This was Chris Cochran kissing her! She would have known it was him even if she'd been wearing a blindfold because of the tingling sensation she'd experienced as soon as he touched her. Her body must be some kind of tuning fork where he was concerned!

That was her last coherent thought. Maribeth had thought that she was experienced in the art of kissing at least, but she'd never experienced anything like this before. All she could do was wrap her arms around his waist and hold on.

By the time he drew away from her with obvious reluctance some untold time later, she was having trouble getting her breath. He seemed to be having a similar problem. He leaned his forehead against hers.

"So what do you say?" he whispered. "Shall we shock everybody and do it?"

She was already in shock, and all she'd done was kiss Chris Cochran. Perhaps it would be better to say that Chris had kissed her.

Her head was still swimming.

In a few short hours everything she thought she knew and understood about herself and her life had been turned upside down. She'd been grieving over Bobby one minute and wholeheartedly participating in a kiss with Chris the next.

Had the whole world gone mad, or was it just her?

"Oh, Chris. I can't make a decision like that right now. I can't even *think* right now."

He couldn't see her face, but he could hear the pain and confusion in her voice. He wasn't certain what to say. He knew better than to kiss her again. That way led to madness if he couldn't place her on the blanket nearby and make passionate love to her.

"I need to get back home," she said, only now stepping away from him. "Everybody will be wondering why I've been gone so long."

"You're twenty-six years old, Maribeth, not sixteen. Believe it or not, you don't have to account for every moment of your life anymore."

"You're right, of course. I guess it's a habit."

"I sometimes wonder if you don't feel as though you're in some kind of suspended time frame, like

Sleeping Beauty, waiting for your prince to come claim you. You've been content to stay here with your family working on the ranch while you waited for Bobby to return home.''

"Perhaps. I don't know. I've stayed here because this has been my life. I never envisioned another kind. There was no reason to, until now. I never would have guessed that Bobby would do something like this. I knew he wasn't in any hurry to come home, which is why I didn't push him to set a date for the wedding. After four years on the road, I thought he was getting ready to settle down. How could I have known...?'' Her voice trailed off, leaving her feeling so empty. The life she thought she'd had was no longer there. What could she do to create an alternate future? The thought was scary, no matter what she chose.

"Come with me, Maribeth. Give me the opportunity to show you what's out there on the horizon. Will you do that for me... and for yourself?''

"I don't know, Chris. Everything is happening at once. This must be how a person would feel when they're enjoying the scenic countryside and then suddenly step on a land mine. My world's just exploded into little pieces.''

He kissed her again, a gentle, soothing touch that still set all her senses on red alert.

"Give me the chance to help put your life back together, will you?'' he murmured. "I don't want to leave here with you feeling so shattered.''

"And how do I explain the switch to people?''

"It's too late to say much, isn't it? If you agree to marry me, you don't really need to make any explanations. Everyone will come to see you get married as planned. You'll still be getting married. Only the groom will be different.''

"You don't think they'll notice?" she asked, almost laughing at the idea. "Chris, this isn't some kind of play where suddenly the understudy has to fill in."

"Maybe not, but it would certainly give the people in the county something to talk about for years to come."

"Oh, Chris, how could I have forgotten your crazy sense of humor?"

"If you'll marry me, you'll be able to stay in closer touch to be reminded."

"I must be out of my mind. I'm actually considering the idea."

That was as much as he could hope for. He didn't want to push his luck. "Why don't I take you home? You're exhausted and still in shock. I'll spend the night at my family's place and we'll talk tomorrow. See how you feel about things then. A good night's sleep will do wonders for you."

"I'm not sure I could sleep. I don't know how I could get my mind to slow down. It seems to be running off in all directions."

He gathered up the blanket and led her back to the car. Once inside, he took her hand. "I just want you to remember that you don't have to deal with this on your own. I'm here for you. I want to help. You know that I'll accept whatever you decide, but I want you to consider my offer. Will you do that for me?"

Her face was a pale blur in the dark. He couldn't read her expression. "I can't believe you'd be willing to make such a sacrifice."

"Sacrifice?"

"Marrying me."

His laugh was self-mocking even though she wasn't aware of it. "Someday I hope to convince you that marrying you is definitely not my idea of a sacrifice."

He started the car and backed around, taking the road back to the highway. He was encouraged by the fact that she had left her hand in his. It remained there all the way back to the ranch.

"Well, there you are," Megan said when Maribeth walked into the house. "I was wondering if we needed to send out a search party for you."

Maribeth kept her head down, hoping Megan wouldn't notice her face. She still clutched Chris's handkerchief in her hand.

"We just got to talking," she replied, her voice sounding hoarse in her ears, "and didn't notice the time."

They were in the kitchen and Maribeth opened the refrigerator as though looking for something to eat.

"Well, it's a good thing Bobby's not the jealous type. Otherwise he might have something to say about his fiancée disappearing for hours with his best friend." When Maribeth continued to stare sightlessly into the refrigerator, Megan added, "I saved you a plate. It's on the bottom shelf."

"Thanks." Maribeth's reply was muffled.

"Are you getting a cold? You sound funny." Megan took the plate out of Maribeth's hands and looked at her. "And your face is all blotchy. Have you been crying?"

"For Pete's sake, Megan. I'm twenty-six years old. I don't need you mothering me any longer. Would you give it a rest?"

Megan blinked in surprise. Maribeth knew she was acting out of character, but she wasn't ready to discuss the news she'd received with anyone at the moment. For that matter, she couldn't imagine a time when she'd be ready to tell the family that Bobby Metcalf had cared so little for her that he had blithely run off and married somebody else days before their wedding.

She watched Megan put the plate of food in the microwave and set the timer. The silence in the kitchen became oppressive to her.

"I'm sorry I snapped at you," Maribeth finally said, sitting down at the table and gently rubbing her swollen eyelids. "My eyes have been watering. I guess I could be getting a cold."

Megan poured a glass of iced tea and set it down in front of her. "At the risk of sounding too motherly once again, I'd suggest that you take a hot bath after dinner and get to bed early. You certainly don't want to be coughing and sneezing on Saturday."

The microwave pinged and Maribeth jumped up to get there first. "Good idea. I think I'll do that," she muttered, carrying her plate and silverware to the table.

"Do you want me to stay with you while you eat?"

Maribeth knew that her sister was just trying to be polite. Normally Maribeth would have enjoyed her company. But not now. Now, all she wanted was to be left alone.

"That's okay, sis. But thanks for the offer." She kept her eyes on her food.

Once Megan left the kitchen Maribeth tried her best to eat. She knew she couldn't choke down much of it, but Megan's attitude was just a small sample of what she could expect, magnified a few dozen times, if she told her family what had happened. She could almost visualize what would happen. Megan would immediately get on the phone to Mollie. Then her sisters would tell their husbands. She wouldn't put it past Travis and Deke to round up a posse of angry friends and neighbors and go after Bobby with the intention of lynching him.

Even the children would get into the act in their own way—trying to comfort her with pats and special little gifts.

How could she possibly deal with all of that? Chris was right. She needed to get away from here. Maybe she *would* leave for a while. She could go anywhere. She'd been faithfully saving the money Travis paid her, knowing she'd need money once she and Bobby were married. She could take the money and go to Houston, or maybe San Antonio... or Dallas.

Of course, she could go to Dallas without actually living with Chris. At least he would be there close by. She could find an apartment, maybe find a job somewhere. She could—

Just who was she fooling? She'd never been on her own in her life! She'd always had friends and family around her, looking after her, caring for her, babying her.

The truth was that she'd been spoiled by everyone. She barely remembered her parents. What stood out in her memory from that awful time was how upset Megan and Mollie had been. It was only later that she understood that the three of them could have been split up and put into foster homes.

None of those memories seemed real to her now. She'd grown up with Mollie taking care of the house and meals and Megan working the ranch.

What, exactly, had she contributed to the group?

A big fat zero.

She'd blithely played with her friends, tagged along behind Bobby and Chris, worked with her 4-H projects and planned her future around Bobby Metcalf.

It was almost as if Bobby's actions had forced her to stop and take a cold, hard look at herself.

She didn't like what she saw.

By the time Megan and Mollie had reached her age, they were wives and mothers, running households, being responsible.

She was still playing with her animals and getting paid for it.

Maribeth looked down at her plate and realized that she'd eaten every bite of food on it. So much for all the agonized suffering she was doing. It certainly hadn't affected her appetite.

What she was doing was sitting there feeling sorry for herself, feeling picked on because she had a sister who was concerned about her, knowing how the family would rally around her if she told them the truth.

What she needed to do was to grow up...and Chris had offered her a way to do that. She could marry him, even though her family would never understand it, and she could set out to prove to herself and everyone else that she was an adult.

The fact was she *was* a coward. She didn't want anyone in Agua Verde to know what Bobby had done, especially while she lived there. She didn't think she could face any of them knowing how easily she'd been duped.

There was no way she could make a decision tonight. Tonight she would take Megan's advice. This was her reality, whether she liked it or not. Maribeth O'Brien was not going to marry Bobby Metcalf, despite all her hopes, her plans, her dreams. It was not going to happen.

Now she had to decide what she intended to do with the rest of her life.

A sudden memory of Chris's kiss flashed into her mind and she shivered. What she had felt stunned her. She had kissed Bobby many times and had enjoyed it, but his kisses had never affected her the way the one Chris had given her.

Just thinking about it made her body react in a new, unexpected way.

She was shaken by the realization that she wanted it to happen again.

Three

"**I** don't see how you can stand there looking so calm," Megan said to Maribeth with mounting exasperation three days later. "Haven't you heard a thing Mollie's been saying to you?"

Maribeth studied her pale reflection in the full-length mirror, deliberately concentrating on her image in an effort to remain as calm as Megan thought she was. She was too pale. Weren't brides supposed to be glowing or something? Her hair was the only thing about her giving off any color. Her eyes, wider than normal, stared back at her.

Who was this woman? She didn't recognize her at all. She fingered the veil. From this distance it looked like a cloud hovering around her head.

An appropriate piece of symbolism.

Obviously she'd had her head in a cloud for years, ignoring what had been happening between her and Bobby, refusing to deal with the reality of her life.

She was tired of passively waiting for her life to begin. She was ready to plan an entirely new one, away from Agua Verde and everything that was familiar to her.

Her decisions had brought her to this place at this time. The three sisters now waited in a small room off the foyer of the church they had attended all their lives. Her wedding was set to begin in another few minutes. A wedding without the designated bridegroom.

"I heard her," she finally replied, her eyes still focused on the image in the mirror while her thoughts were elsewhere.

"Don't you understand what this means?" Megan asked, her voice wobbling just a little. "Nobody, and I mean absolutely no one in this town, has seen Bobby Metcalf this morning. Having Chris fill in for him at the rehearsal last night is one thing, but if he doesn't appear in the next few minutes, you're going to look foolish walking down that aisle and not having a groom waiting. Time is running out. What are you going to do, Mary Elizabeth? Now's the time to call off the ceremony, before you actually walk down that aisle." Megan was actually wringing her hands.

Of course Megan was right. She could still call off the ceremony right now if she wanted. No one was forcing her to marry Chris, even though they had gotten their marriage license the day after he arrived, swearing the clerk to strict secrecy until after the ceremony. Not wanting to test the restraint of the small town's gossip mill any further, Chris had driven to Fredericksburg to get her a wedding band yesterday.

Was she out of her mind? Had the shock been too much for her? Or was Chris's offer too tempting to resist? At the moment, she didn't have a clue.

"Oh, leave her alone, Megan," Mollie said. "If the bride isn't concerned, why should you be?"

Maribeth almost laughed at the absurdity of the situation. Concerned? She was terrified! Of her own choices, her judgment or lack thereof, of the future, of breaking down in front of all of these people and admitting that she was a complete fraud—that Bobby Metcalf thought so little of her that he hadn't bothered to get in touch with her directly after marrying someone else.

She wasn't sure she could have gotten through the past three days without Chris. He'd been very matter-of-fact when she told him she would marry him, making arrangements for the license and ring. He'd even laughed when she told him she hadn't told anyone that Bobby wasn't going to be there.

He'd carried off his role of substitute groom at the rehearsal with a casual acceptance of the situation, so that everyone else in the wedding party had accepted Bobby's absence with little more than raised brows and questioning looks at one another.

Megan went over to one of the folding chairs lined up along the wall and threw herself into the chair. "I swear, I'm going to have gray hair before this day is over."

"Megan! You're going to crush your dress," Mollie said, shaking her head in exasperation. "Do you realize that you're acting more like a nervous bride than Maribeth is? You didn't act this hyper when you and Travis got married!"

Megan ran her hand nervously over her dress. "Well, at least Travis was at the church when it was time to get married! Do *you* realize that the chapel is crammed full of people, waiting for us to start this thing? And does your sister care? Oh, no. She's just been humming to herself all morning, as though she didn't have a care in the world.''

Maribeth turned away from the mirror and looked over at her oldest sister. "Everything's going to turn out all right," she said, "Please don't be upset, Megan."

Mollie leaned over and straightened the train on Maribeth's gown. "Well, if no one else is going to comment, I guess it's up to me. I think you make a beautiful bride, Maribeth," Mollie said.

"Thanks to you," she replied, hugging Mollie. "At least I didn't have to worry about finding a wedding dress." She glanced back into the mirror. "I'm glad that each of us wore the same dress. I remember watching you make it, Mollie, when Megan got married. I was so excited, thinking about the day that I would be wearing it, too."

Maribeth forced herself to keep playing the role of the ecstatic bride for just a few more hours. She'd discovered a hitherto unknown talent for acting in the past three days.

"I think it's time to—" she began just as someone tapped on the door.

"Maybe Bobby's arrived," Mollie said, hurrying to the door.

As soon as she opened it, Travis peeked inside, saying, "I just got the signal. We're ready to begin. You ladies better get out here, so I can escort the bride down the aisle."

Megan jumped up at the sound of her husband's voice. "Oh, good. Bobby's here, then," she said, joining Mollie at the door.

"All I know is that Chris and the pastor signaled that it was time to start," Travis replied.

Mollie picked up the bridal bouquet and handed it to Maribeth, then kissed her on the cheek. "Here we go, sweetie. I'm getting Megan out of here before she has a heart attack."

Travis must have heard her, because he was chuckling when Maribeth joined him at the door. They could hear the organ pause, then begin the music that was the signal for her sisters to start down the aisle. Only then did Travis look at her and say, "Exactly what are you up to, baby sister?"

She tried to meet his steady gaze, but couldn't hold it. "I don't know what you mean."

"I mean that Bobby is not here and you're not at all surprised. It's my guess that you would be shocked if he were to suddenly show up."

"Fat chance," she muttered under her breath.

"So what's this all about?"

She glanced around the foyer. There was no one there. Everyone was inside waiting for her entrance. Oh, what the heck. It was too late to back out now. She could tell him something of the truth.

"I've decided to take charge of my life."

That certainly got his attention. He stared at her in bewilderment. "What are you talking about?"

She sighed, trying to find the words that would make some sense to him. "I'm leaving home, Travis. It's past time, don't you think? You created a job for me so I wouldn't feel quite so useless around the ranch, but the truth is you don't need me there."

"Has all this wedding hoopla been too much for you, honey? I swear you're not making a lick o' sense. What does your working for me—and you do a damn fine job,

I might add—have to do with your bridegroom not showing up?''

"There's our cue. It's time to go," she hurriedly whispered.

She adjusted the veil so that it was over her eyes. She had no trouble seeing, and the netting made a great camouflage for her expression.

The chapel was small. As soon as she stepped into the doorway she saw Chris in a tuxedo standing beside the pastor, both of them watching for her entrance. In that moment, Maribeth felt she was seeing Chris Cochran, the man, for the first time.

He was taller than the pastor by almost a head, probably around six feet tall, with broad shoulders tapering to a slim waist and narrow hips, his long, muscular legs slightly apart and braced.

She'd always taken his dark good looks for granted. Until now. His black-eyed gaze met and held hers. The light from the frosted windows above him emphasized his dark hair, high cheekbones and strong jawline. He was a stranger to her. There was so much she didn't know about him.

How could she possibly be considering marriage to him?

At that moment she saw a tiny muscle in his jaw jump, and she realized that he was as nervous as she was. That made her feel a little better.

They both might be out of their minds for jumping into this, but they were in it together. She made a silent vow to do everything in her power to make their relationship work, starting now. No matter what he said, Chris was giving up a great deal to help her through a bad time in her life. She didn't ever want him to regret his out-of-character impulsiveness.

Maribeth kept her eyes on Chris, although she could feel the gaze of everyone upon her. No doubt they were wondering if she was too nearsighted to notice that the prospective groom was conspicuous by his absence at the front of the church.

She waited until she and Travis had almost reached the altar before whispering, "Would you fill in as Chris's best man?"

Travis glanced down at her in surprise, then looked at Chris who was watching them with narrowed eyes. As usual, Travis was quick to grasp a situation. With a slight squeeze of her hand and a brief nod he escorted her to where the pastor and Chris stood, then stepped back.

There wasn't a sound in the chapel. As far as she could tell, everyone there was holding his and her collective breath, no doubt waiting for her to become hysterical at the sudden realization that Bobby Metcalf had failed to materialize.

Chris stepped forward and firmly took her hand in his.

Maribeth heard several gasps from behind her. Good. They were bound to need air by this time.

"Dearly beloved," the pastor intoned, and began the service as though nothing at all was out of the ordinary. But then he'd been informed of the change as soon as Chris arrived at the church that morning.

When the pastor asked who offered the bride, Travis quietly replied, "Her sisters and me," with such sincerity and love that Maribeth suddenly had a lump in her throat.

Then, as though it had all been rehearsed, Travis stepped over and stood beside Chris instead of returning to the seat reserved for him. She saw Chris slip something into Travis's hand . . . no doubt her wedding band.

So far, so good.

Maribeth found herself holding her breath when the pastor asked if there was anyone present who could give good cause why the two of them should not wed, and if so, to speak now. From the corner of her eye, she glanced at Megan who stood beside her. She wouldn't put it past her sister to interrupt the ceremony right then and there to demand an explanation. Instead Megan stood staring at the pastor as though watching a white rabbit perform tricks. She obviously didn't know what to expect next.

Only silence greeted the ritualistic question and Maribeth was able to breathe once again.

At the appropriate time Travis calmly offered Chris the ring to slip on her finger. She hadn't seen it until now. It was beautiful—a broad band of intricately carved gold that glowed with a burnished gleam in the suffused light.

She smiled at him when he slipped it onto her finger.

After Chris repeated his vows, the pastor requested the ring she was to put on Chris's finger be presented. But she hadn't bought him a ring! They hadn't discussed it.

Before she could think of what to do, Chris unobtrusively slipped a ring into the palm of her hand, a matching one to the one she now wore.

Startled, she looked at him. His dark eyes held hers with a steady gaze as he held out his hand to her. With trembling fingers she carefully eased the ring over his knuckles while repeating the vows.

Maribeth had never been so aware of another human being in her life as she was of Chris at that moment. She felt as though more than hands had been linked, more than words had been spoken. Something had passed between them, a sense of unity that no mere ceremony could have caused.

"I now pronounce you husband and wife," the pastor said, smiling. To Chris he said, "You may kiss the bride."

She turned to Chris. This part hadn't been rehearsed the night before. This time everything was for real. Even the kiss.

Chris took his time carefully folding the veil back from her face. With a gentleness that continued to startle her, a gentleness she would never have expected from this man, he slipped his arm around her waist and tilted her chin slightly upward with his other hand.

"Hello, Mrs. Cochran," he whispered. "Welcome to my world."

His lips felt warm and even softer than she remembered as he brushed them, oh, so lightly, across hers.

She couldn't seem to control the trembling that suddenly overtook her. She felt flushed and fought the inexplicable urge to cry. When he released her, he took her hand, holding it firmly in his.

When the pastor turned them and introduced Mr. and Mrs. Christopher Cochran to the congregation, she saw that she wasn't the only one experiencing an acute sense of shock and bewilderment.

The triumphant recessional music began and Chris took her arm. By the time they reached the church foyer Maribeth felt surrounded by a sea of people. She leaned against Chris, who immediately wrapped both arms around her, holding her closely against his chest.

She felt light-headed and very strange. She'd never compared the two men before, but now she realized how physically different Bobby and Chris were. Bobby was shorter and more compact, only a few inches taller than she. Standing this close to Chris, Maribeth noticed that the top of her head barely cleared his chin. He was a much larger man than Bobby, his shoulders wider.

She allowed her head to rest against his chest, feeling a sense of protection that was new to her. Through the expensive material of his suit she could feel the rapid beat of his heart. Once again, his outward calm was deceptive. She'd never known anyone so good at hiding what he was feeling.

She wished she knew how he did it. "I'm not at all certain I'm going to be able to carry this off much longer," she murmured beneath the sounds around them. "My knees are shaking so hard I can scarcely stand."

Chris brushed his lips against her neck in a very loverlike expression of affection. "Would you like for me to carry you across the street to the reception? I think my back's up to the job." She could hear the amusement in his voice, even though his expression remained suitably solemn.

That was all either of them had time to say before the crowd began to press in around them, seemingly all talking at once.

Maribeth was glad that the O'Brien sisters had decided to hold the reception at the community center, which was directly across the street from the church. She was in the midst of trying to explain to Chris that she was fairly certain she could walk that far when he suddenly swooped her up into his arms, causing another ripple of reaction in those around them.

Glancing at the gathering crowd he said, "Shall we adjourn this meeting across the street?" Without waiting for a response, he left the church with Maribeth in his arms. She clung to him, almost grateful for his decisive action. For this moment, at least, nothing more was expected of her than to hang on to him.

"The sooner we cut the cake," he murmured into her ear, "the sooner we can get out of here. I don't know about you, but I'm more than ready to blow this pop stand." The smile he gave her was an intimate one, as though he had already determined what he would prefer to be doing at the moment.

She could feel her face heating up. What in the world was wrong with her, anyway? This was someone she'd known for years. Why was she having such a strong, physical reaction to him when she'd never felt that way toward anyone before?

She laughed a little shakily. "I can't believe we actually went through with it," she replied, looking back over his shoulder at the people continuing to stream out of the church and follow them. "Have you ever seen so many expressions of shock on people's faces? It's quite possible Megan may never forgive me for this."

"Sure she will. It's your life, after all. Besides, everybody needs a little shake up every once in a while. Keeps a person out of a rut."

"Well, I think I've been tossed out of my rut quite adequately this week, thank you very much. I'm really not the adventurous type, you know."

Chris chuckled, allowing her feet to touch the ground once again. "Stick with me, kid, and you'll find it gets easier as you go along." They walked into the decorated community center, which was rapidly filling with family and guests. A small combo was playing in one corner. The music was soft and unobtrusive.

"The place looks great. Did you help with the decorations?" Chris asked.

"I think half the women in town were here, volunteering their services. One of Mollie's friends made the bridal cake, someone else brought the punch."

"Well, I guess it's time for us to face everyone. Are you up for the receiving line?"

"Let's hope. I'll just be glad when today is over and done with."

"Hey, don't wish away your wedding day, Mrs. Cochran. It's supposed to be a happy occasion." He placed a tiny kiss on her temple. "I want you to be happy, Maribeth."

She closed her eyes, inhaling his distinctive after-shave. She went up on tiptoes and kissed his jaw. "Thank you, Chris. For everything you've done for me."

His eyes seemed to be filled with mysterious glints when he smiled at her. "Believe me. The pleasure has been all mine."

Megan rushed up to them. "C'mon, y'all, you've got to get into the receiving line. This whole affair has been crazy enough without forgetting to greet people coming in." She moved off, muttering something about darned kids. For some reason Maribeth didn't think she was referring to her own offspring.

Maribeth exchanged a glance with Chris who grinned back at her. He was right. This *was* her wedding day. It wasn't the one she'd expected to have, and Chris certainly wasn't the man she'd thought would be standing by her side. Nevertheless, the deed was now done. It was too late for regrets or second thoughts. It was time to celebrate the union.

Maribeth tucked her arm through his and said, "We might as well go face all the curious stares. I wonder if anyone is brave enough to demand explanations?"

"There's only one way to find out. Shall we go?"

She and Chris received many blessings and well-wishes from friends in the next hour. No one was impolite enough to actually ask what happened to Bobby Metcalf, whose name had been on the wedding invitations, but several admitted to being surprised at the way things had turned out.

However, it was Travis who summed up everyone's attitude when he paused long enough in the line to give Maribeth an exuberant kiss before shaking Chris's hand and solemnly asking, "The groom, I presume?" which caused a great deal of nervous laughter.

Chris thanked him for filling in as best man, but Travis waved his thanks away. "Hey, I was glad to be of some help. Maribeth has continued to be a source of surprise to this entire family on more than one occasion. I don't know why we should be surprised that she'd pull off something like this."

Maribeth began to relax after that, believing the worst was behind them. She saw Chris's mother and grandparents come in after the receiving line had disbanded. She took Chris's hand and led him over to greet them.

"I'm so glad you came to the wedding today, Mrs. Cochran, Mr. and Mrs. Lambert. I suppose Chris told you about our plans before you came."

His grandmother was the first to speak. "At first I didn't really believe he was serious, Maribeth. I suppose that's one reason I had to come today. Not that I wouldn't have wanted to see you get married and all, but I haven't been getting out much lately."

Maribeth could see how frail the older woman had become since she'd seen her last. She carefully hugged her. "I'm so glad you managed to be here."

His grandfather didn't say much. He just awkwardly patted her hand, shook Chris's hand, then helped his wife to one of the chairs arranged nearby.

Maribeth turned to say something to Chris's mother, but found her already in conversation with him. "I don't know why I should have been surprised by your actions," she was saying in a low, caustic voice. "You are your father's son, after all. It must be gratifying to grab the prettiest girl in the county away from your best friend. I tried my best to raise you with some kind of morals and a sense of ethics, but I can't fight genetics."

Maribeth glanced at Chris, surprised at the venom in the woman's voice. This was her only child she was talking to, after all. His face registered no response to her words. He looked at her as politely, as impassively, as he'd greeted everyone there.

Maribeth couldn't just stand by and let his mother think so wrongly about Chris. He'd done nothing wrong. His actions had been highly honorable. "Mrs. Cochran, you don't understand. Chris was—"

"Don't explain," he said, firmly cutting off her words. "It doesn't matter." To his mother, he said, "Thank you for coming despite your feelings."

"I wouldn't have come if I'd thought there was a chance your father might be here. You assured me he wouldn't be."

"That's right. He doesn't know about the sudden switch in my plans. When I left Dallas on Wednesday, I was coming down to be Bobby's best man. I haven't spoken to him since then."

She looked amused. "It was smart of you to marry her before your dad gets a glimpse of her. Otherwise, he might have tried to snap her up himself." As though feeling the need to explain her remark to Maribeth, she smiled brilliantly at her and said, "You see, Chris's father trades in wives like most men trade in their cars— always for a newer, flashier model. So far, Chris seems to be determined to be just like his father with his fancy cars and his fancy women."

Maribeth almost choked in surprise. "Are you talking about me?" she asked. "I'm the last person to be considered fancy."

"You can't help being what you are, Maribeth. You've always been beautiful. You can't be anything else. I'm sure Chris is going to enjoy showing you off to all his rich, snobbish friends...until he gets bored. Being his father's son, that won't take long."

"Let it go, Mother, okay? I've been married a little more than an hour. Try not to make too many predictions about the future of my marriage at this stage. Who knows? Maybe I'll surprise you." He glanced around. "The photographer is waiting for us to cut the cake so he can finish getting pictures. Would you like to join us at the head table?"

"No. I'll sit with the folks. They aren't going to want to stay long."

Chris hugged his mother. "I'll be in touch." He took Maribeth's hand and led her to the head table.

She looked over her shoulder at his mother. "Chris, don't you think we should—"

"There's nothing we can do, Maribeth. I know her attitude must seem strange to you, being raised in the kind of family you have. I'll explain later."

There was no more time for talk. Once again, they were caught up in the traditional routines of a wedding celebration.

The photographer took pictures as they cut the cake and fed each other a bite. Then Mollie took over and helped them pass out pieces of the tasty confection to each guest.

Toasts were made and the traditional first dance was performed, Maribeth nervously following Chris's lead.

"I don't know how to dance," she murmured when he took her out on the dance floor with everyone watching.

"Something else I can teach you how to do," he replied with a wicked glint in his eye. He wrapped his arm firmly around her waist and guided her through the simple steps that kept time to the music.

His words successfully distracted her from her self-consciousness. "Something else?"

"Mmm-hmm."

"What else do you intend to teach me?"

He grinned. "Oh, I don't know. I'll try to think of something."

"Are you trying to say that you have more experience than I have?"

"In some things. Perhaps."

"Perhaps! Are we talking about what your mama warned you no gentleman talks about?"

He began to laugh. "Ah, Maribeth. What a delight you are. You have made me a very happy man."

"I have?"

"Oh, yes. I will be forever grateful to Bobby Metcalf for stepping aside and leaving the field open for me."

"Grateful! How could you possibly feel that Bobby's behavior could be—"

"We'll talk about it later...say, on the ride to San Antonio."

"San Antonio? I thought we were going to Dallas?"

"I'm a little embarrassed to have to admit that as soon as we're through here, I have to get back to work. I forgot about that when we were talking earlier this week. Not that my working would have stopped me from marrying you. It's just that you're going to get an immediate taste of what my life is like."

She could hear a rueful acceptance in his voice that she'd not heard before.

"I don't understand."

"Another thing to discuss on our way. At least our life together won't be boring, right?"

Then it was time for more photographs. This time the groom was to remove the bride's garter and toss it to the male guests.

He took his own sweet time about removing it from her thigh. "Chris!" she hissed. "For Pete's sake, hurry up." Her words created a great deal of laughter and ribald remarks about her impatience. From the look in his eyes as he grinned at her while kneeling in front of her, he knew exactly why she was bothered.

Maribeth lived in jeans. She wasn't used to wearing dresses, or hose, or garters. And she certainly wasn't used to having a man slide his fingers along her calf, her knee and her inner thigh. His touch was causing strange sensations all over her body. Her breasts were tingling and butterflies had lodged in her stomach.

She was relieved when he finally retrieved the garter and blithely tossed it over his shoulder. He stood, grabbed her in his arms and gave her a robust kiss, much to the delight and applause of those watching.

"Throw the bouquet!" was the next directive.

In moments the single women were gathered in front of her. She tossed it high in the air, but didn't see who caught it because Chris whisked her back onto the dance floor. "They're playing our song," he explained, gathering her into his arms.

"We don't have a song, you idiot!" she managed to gasp when she'd caught her breath.

He sighed in contentment after aligning her body to his. "We do now." Both of his arms were wrapped around her waist, so that she had no choice but to rest her hands on his chest.

"How much champagne have you had today?" she asked suspiciously.

"None. I never drink when I know I'm going to be flying."

"Is that what you meant about going to work?"

"Mmm. One of the company planes is in San Antonio. I'm flying it back to Dallas tonight, so that it will be ready to leave tomorrow."

"You're leaving tomorrow?"

"Unless I can get another pilot to take it. We rotate, and it's my turn."

"Where will you be going?"

"Atlanta...then Miami. My dad does considerable business in that area."

"Oh."

"I figure either place is as good a spot for a honeymoon as anywhere else."

"Then you can take me with you?"

"That's right. Or I'm not going."

"But what about your car?"

"One of the mechanics will get it back to Dallas for me. Believe me, they won't find it a hardship."

"Oh."

She'd wanted a different life, hadn't she? Well, that was what she was getting. Whenever she'd considered her postmarriage plans she'd seen herself in Dallas, finding a job, brushing up on her cooking skills, waiting for Chris to come home. It only now occurred to her that he might not have a nine-to-five occupation.

He glanced around at all the other couples now taking the floor. "Do you think we can sneak away for you to change out of that dress? I think you'll be more comfortable in something a little less formal for the flight back.''

She, too, glanced around. "I don't think anyone is going to miss us.'' They took their time leaving the dance floor, stopping to speak to several couples, but eventually they were able to slip out a side door.

"Where are your clothes?'' Chris asked, standing on the curb. It was almost dark and the streetlights offered circles of light along the street.

"At the church. I'll go over and change. I won't be long.''

"Do you need some help?''

Before she could answer both Megan and Mollie joined them. "We thought you might need help changing out of that dress,'' Mollie said, smiling.

"Yeah, I distinctly remember it took two people to get out of it,'' Megan said, obviously amused about something.

Maribeth and Chris exchanged glances and she shrugged. "Thanks. It would probably save time.'' She didn't see why Megan found that remark funny, but Megan laughed and agreed with her.

"Deke hid your car at our place,'' Mollie said. "He should be back with it any minute.'' She eyed her new brother-in-law ruefully. "Here we thought you were being so generous, loaning your car to Bobby and Maribeth. Little did we know.''

Chris didn't bat an eye at her teasing admonishment. "I appreciate y'all taking care of it for me.''

They heard the sound of a high-powered engine coming slowly toward them. Deke drove up in Chris's car and paused by the group standing by the side of the street. He double-parked and got out of the car. "What's the matter? Am I late?''

"Not at all," Chris assured him. "Maribeth needs to change before we can take off. Your timing couldn't be better."

"That is one sweet baby to drive," Deke admitted, giving him the keys. "Thanks for letting me have the opportunity to drive it."

The three women left the men talking cars and engine performance and hurried into the church, where Maribeth had stored the summer dress she'd intended to wear once the ceremony was over. She wished now that she'd opted for her jeans. She needed something that was familiar to her.

She also knew that she wasn't going to escape the questions and comments any longer, now that her sisters had gotten her alone.

They didn't disappoint her.

"I just hope you know what you're doing," Mollie began the subject while she quickly unbuttoned the back of the gown.

"Me, too," Maribeth replied with devout sincerity.

After a lengthy silence that led her to believe they weren't going to make any other comments, Megan suddenly spoke up.

"What did you do with Bobby, anyway?" Her tone couldn't have sounded more casual.

Maribeth could feel her cheeks going red. "I didn't do anything with him, for Pete's sake! What in the world do you think I would have done with him?"

Mollie helped her to step out of her gown while Megan handed Maribeth her dress, then helped her slide her arms through the sleeves before answering.

"You can't really blame me for wondering, can you? After all, you've talked about marrying Bobby Metcalf for years. And yet I just watched you marry Chris Cochran despite all your plans. Pardon me for being confused about what's going on.''

All right. So she owed them an explanation. What did it matter, anyway? The deed was done. Nobody was going to talk her out of her decision now. Was that what she had been afraid of? How strange.

Maribeth found her other shoes and put them on, then began to pull the pins out of her hair. Megan and Mollie watched her in silence.

''Do you remember when Chris stopped by the ranch on Wednesday?'' she finally asked, brushing her hair out, then absently braiding it into her usual thick plait.

Megan was the first to answer. ''You mean when you stayed out with him until all hours? Of course I remember. I should have known something was up then, shouldn't I?''

Maribeth turned away from the mirror and sat down in one of the chairs. She motioned for her sisters to join her. ''Chris came down from Dallas to tell me that Bobby had called him the night before from Las Vegas. It seems that Bobby suddenly got the urge to elope. So he did. I never found out who the bride turned out to be. I just know it wasn't me.''

Her sisters stared at her as though they'd been caught in suspended animation. She looked at each of them before glancing down at her fingers, which were nervously toying with her belt. ''Chris offered to step in and become the groom. After thinking it over, I took him up on his offer.''

Mollie was the first one to find her voice. ''But, Maribeth! Why didn't you tell us? Why would you decide to jump into a new relationship rather than face what had happened between you and Bobby? It certainly wasn't your fault that Bobby did something so crazy. It seems to me that you've just compounded the problem, impulsively jumping into marriage with somebody you don't know.''

"I know Chris,'' Maribeth immediately replied, knowing she sounded defensive, but not being able to help it. "I know him as well as I know Bobby.''

"I guess that isn't saying all that much, now, is it?'' Megan drawled. "I thought you were happy living with us. I had no idea you were so desperate to leave home that you'd go to such lengths to get away.''

Maribeth jumped up from her chair and knelt beside Megan. She couldn't stop the tears that suddenly filled her eyes when she hugged Megan.

"Please don't take what I've done personally, Megan. Please. You know I love you and Travis and the kids. It's just that it's past time for me to be out on my own. I—''

"Out on your own!'' Megan repeated incredulously. "Is that what you think you've done? Honey, I don't know quite how to break the news to you, but you'd better think again. You are Christopher Cochran's wife. You are not out on your own.''

"I know. It's just that—''

"Don't you have any idea who his family is?''

"Well, his mother—''

"No. I don't mean his mother. I'm talking about Kenneth Cochran.'' Megan shook her head. "I don't think you have a clue what you're going to find as the daughter-in-law of Kenneth Cochran. That man moves in some pretty high-and-mighty circles. And you've never even met him, have you?''

"No, but what difference does that make?''

Mollie patted her hand, then pulled her to her feet. "Hopefully everything is going to work out just fine for you, Maribeth. All we want for you is your happiness. You know that, don't you?"

Once again Maribeth's eyes filled with tears as she and Mollie hugged.

They pulled away at the sound of a knock on the door. It was Chris. "Maribeth? Are you about ready to go?"

She looked at her sisters, then at the door. The time had come for her to take her first step away from her family and toward her future. She wasn't ready. Suddenly she knew that.

All Maribeth wanted to do at the moment was to be twelve years old again, feeling safe and secure with her sisters.

She swallowed. "Sorry to keep you waiting, Chris," she said, opening the door. Her voice sounded a little ragged, but she couldn't help it. She turned to Megan and Mollie. "I've gotta go." She hugged each of them one more time. "I'll give you a call soon. I promise. Things are going to work all right. I know they will."

She turned back to Chris, who stood in the doorway watching her with a sympathetic smile on his face, just as though he knew how difficult this moment was for her. However, his voice sounded light when he asked, "Ready?"

She nodded, suddenly unable to make a sound.

"Good. I moved the car around to the back, but we're pushing our luck the longer we stay. I have horrible visions of my car covered with streamers and the windows soaped with messages."

She turned back to her sisters. "Thanks for everything. You've been wonderful. I'm going to miss you."

Megan shooed them out the door. "I know, I know, for all of two minutes. Call us and tell us where you'll be, give us a phone number or an address so we won't feel that you've dropped off the face of the earth."

"I will." She turned to Chris who took her hand and led her down the hallway to one of the doors that led to the back parking lot.

"You okay?" he asked softly.

Thank God it was too dark for him to see her face. "Of course."

"I know it's tough, leaving home for the final time, even when it's the natural cycle of events."

She was glad he understood. But then Chris seemed to understand her very well.

When they pulled out onto the street they found a small group, mostly family, standing on the curb waving. Maribeth waved back until they were out of sight, then slowly turned around in her seat and faced the road.

"I left my packed bags at the ranch. There really isn't much there. I was appalled to discover that everything I own could be packed into two suitcases."

"Don't worry about it. We'll go shopping once we get home."

They reached the ranch and picked up the suitcases that she'd left just inside the kitchen door. Within minutes they were back on the road.

Chris's casual comment kept echoing in her head. *When we get home...* Home. At the moment Maribeth knew that she no longer had a home. Oh, she was sure that eventually she would be able to call Chris's place home. Someday. In the meantime, she had left the O'Brien ranch—the only home she'd ever known—for good.

She looked at Chris, seeing his profile as he watched for the highway that would take them to San Antonio. He was a good man. She knew Megan and Mollie couldn't understand how she could have been so impulsive. After all, both of them had married men they loved and who loved them. She was glad they hadn't questioned her about her feelings for Chris because the truth was, she wasn't at all certain of them.

Today had been filled with all kinds of revelations. Nobody, not even Bobby, had affected her in quite the way Chris did when he gave her a certain look, a look she'd seen more than once today... as though she was a very tempting banquet and he was a starving man.

The look unnerved her and yet... It called to her to find out more. What, exactly, would it be like to be able to satisfy a man's appetite? To fulfill all his intimate longings? The realization that she wanted to find out truly unnerved her. She was tired of wondering about that part of life. She wanted to learn everything that Chris was willing to teach her.

She shivered.

"Are you cold?" he immediately asked, verifying—if she'd had any need—that he was acutely aware of her.

"Oh, no. I'm fine."

"I can turn down the air-conditioning if you'd like."

"No, really. It's quite comfortable."

"If you're sleepy, try to get some rest. We'll be in San Antonio in a couple of hours."

She closed her eyes. Not because she was sleepy, but because she was stunned by her feelings. She was just as aware of Chris as he was of her. Bobby's betrayal had freed her in some very basic way that she wasn't able to understand. He'd hurt her badly. But by his actions Chris had made her feel that Bobby's desertion wasn't the end of the world after all.

Perhaps if she'd had more time, she wouldn't have gone through with this marriage, but at this moment she could not make herself regret it.

Four

Chris interrupted her musing when he reached over and turned on the radio. "I suppose I might as well start confessing now," he said. "You'll find out soon enough."

She glanced at him warily, a little unnerved by his seriousness. "All right," she responded, mentally bracing herself for she knew not what.

"Despite the fact that I was raised deep in the heart of Texas, my musical preference is jazz. Is that going to upset you?"

She rested her head in her palm and groaned. "I thought you were going to tell me something awful!"

"Well, ma'am, confessing that I'm not a fan of country-and-western music is enough to get me run out of the state and my birth certificate revoked. If I'd told you any sooner, you might never have married me."

She shook her head. "I can see that I'm going to have to get used to your weird sense of humor."

"Among other things," he drawled.

"Maybe you'd better tell me about some of those others things so I won't have any more rude surprises."

"Oh, nothing earthshaking. Just your usual, run-of-the-mill habits that people who live together have to get used to in another person. You have to remember that you don't know if I'm messy or neat, whether I'm a morning person or a night person, if I snore, what my favorite meal is, my—"

"All right," she replied, amused by his attitude. "Are you messy or neat? Do you snore? What is your favorite meal?"

He chuckled a little. "Actually I'm fairly neat, but not obsessively so. I'm definitely a morning person, but since I don't need much sleep, I'm fairly late in going to bed. As far as snoring, I really couldn't answer that one."

"What about your favorite meal?"

"A big ol' thick T-bone steak, with lots of French fries and mushrooms."

"That sounds Texan enough for you to be allowed to live here. It also sounds fairly simple. As long as we're confessing our deepest secrets, I guess I never mentioned that I'm not much in the kitchen."

His grin flashed white in the shadows of the car. "Nope. You never did."

"That's because I never had to be. Mollie's the homemaker in the family. I manage to get by." She thought about some of the other things he mentioned. "I'm used to getting up early, but I have to admit that I end up doing things out of habit and not because I'm awake. I don't know about the snoring part."

"Do you have a favorite meal?"

"Not really. I'm willing to eat whatever's there."

They lapsed into silence after that but it was more companionable, somehow. Maribeth felt herself relaxing, the soft music a soothing background to her drifting thoughts. She didn't realize she'd fallen asleep until she opened her eyes when the car slowed down. They were pulling into the gate of an airfield. She straightened and looked around in surprise.

"I must have been more tired than I thought," she said, feeling more than a little self-conscious. "I didn't expect to fall asleep."

"You needed it, I'm sure. You've been under quite a strain these past few days." Although he was obviously speaking to her, Chris's attention was on the airfield. He was looking around the area, his gaze not missing much.

"It hasn't been a picnic for you, either," she murmured. If he heard her, he chose not to comment.

They pulled into a small parking area beside one of the hangars. "It looks like everything's ready for us," he commented. He reached into the back of the car and retrieved his coat jacket and tie. Once out of the car, he tossed the jacket over his shoulder and came around the other side. The lights from the open hangar cast long shadows across him. He leaned over and opened her door.

"I'll get our bags out of the trunk," he said, once she was standing beside him.

"I can help."

Without saying anything more, he opened the trunk and handed her the smallest one, which happened to be his. Then he led the way across the tarmac to the hangar. She had to hurry to keep up with his long-legged stride. "None of these people expect you to have someone with you, do they?"

"It doesn't matter. They work for the company and do what they're told."

Was it her imagination or was there a trace of bitterness in his voice?

"What about your father? Does he care when you take people with you on these trips?"

"You're the first, so it's never come up."

She liked the sound of that and smiled to herself.

When she got a glimpse of the plane Maribeth blinked in surprise. She hadn't been around planes before; in fact, she'd never flown in her life. But the thought didn't frighten her. Instead she was excited to be here.

It was her wedding night, and anything was possible.

Chris placed the luggage inside the plane, a jet that was smaller than the commercial ones she'd seen, but considerably larger than a private plane. He took her hand and led her inside an office where he spoke with two of the men there.

After handing his car keys to one of them, he picked up some papers and they entered the hangar once again.

The plane was now sitting out front. Chris helped her on board. The interior looked like a luxurious lounge. She'd never seen anything like it outside of movies and television. Was this what Megan had meant? Chris seemed to be at home with all of this.

"You can sit wherever you like. It's a short flight. We should be on the ground and on our way to my place within the hour."

She could see that his mind was already on the trip ahead. "I'll be fine. Thanks."

He moved toward the front of the plane, then hesitated. He spun around and in a few quick strides returned to where she had sat down. He leaned over and cupped her face in his hands. "I'd let you up front with me except you're entirely too distracting.'' He gave her a hard, possessive kiss, then quickly retraced his steps, closing the door to the cockpit behind him.

She stared at the closed door, dazed by his sudden, unpredictable behavior. She was quickly learning that there was nothing she knew about Chris that could help her in this situation. There was no trace of the boy she'd once known.

Like it or not, she was married to a stranger. Mysterious, attractive and sexy. *Her husband.*

The flight to Dallas fascinated her. She'd been too enthralled in all the sensations of a first-time flight to be frightened.

Knowing that Chris was at the controls gave an added sense of adventure. She spent the time looking out the porthole window at the lights below, amazed at the number of cities scattered across the landscape.

By the time they landed she was filled with all kinds of questions for Chris. The whole experience had been fun. Who would have believed that she would be flying for the very first time on her wedding day...? Or night, as it was by now. Chris had teased her about teaching her new things, hadn't he?

She felt a little inadequate, actually. There was so much she didn't know. In a way she was glad she'd already confessed her lack of sexual knowledge to Chris. She was so glad that she and Bobby had never been intimate. She didn't think it would have made any difference to Bobby's choices and ultimate behavior, but it would have made his betrayal so much harder for her to bear.

She peered out the window at this larger airfield. When the door from the cockpit opened she was still safely buckled into her seat.

Chris walked over to her. "Well? How was it? Do you think you're going to enjoy flying?" He flipped open her seat belt and helped her to her feet.

"Oh, Chris, it was wonderful! I had no idea that—"

The sound of the outside door opening stopped her. They both glanced around in time to see three men step through the opening.

"Well, son, looks like you made it back from San Antonio just fine," the man in the lead said to Chris.

This must be Kenneth Cochran. He made a very imposing figure. Maribeth could see the family resemblance between the two men—both were tall with dark hair and eyes. There were flashes of gray in the older man's hair. He had a piercing gaze, sizing up the situation and prepared to deal with whatever was going on. He looked like a man who was used to being in control. There was an aura of power about him, enhanced by the expensive suit that must have been tailored for him.

The other two men with him were equally well dressed, no doubt successful businessmen. Each of them carried briefcases as though the bags were extensions of themselves. They probably were.

Chris kept his arm around Maribeth's waist. "I didn't expect you to meet the plane." She'd never heard him sound so cool. "Is this a welcoming committee?" he asked dryly.

The older man showed no reaction to his son's less-than-friendly greeting. "Not at all. Just a slight adjustment in plans. We decided not to wait until morning to go to Atlanta. I've already had them file your flight plan leaving as soon as you're ready to go." Two men dressed in khaki coveralls appeared in the doorway carrying luggage.

Chris glanced at Maribeth before he spoke. "In that case, would it be possible to get someone else to take the flight? I'd made plans on being home tonight."

The smile Kenneth Cochran gave his son wasn't a friendly one. His dark gaze flicked to Maribeth before returning to Chris, his eyes revealing nothing of his thoughts. In a light tone, he said, "Ah, you brought company along, did you? Importing them these days." He stepped closer to them, not missing much about either one of them.

Maribeth had never felt more rustic or uncomfortable in her life. She had a sudden vision of what this sophisticated man must see. She wasn't used to wearing dresses, but Mollie had insisted she start off for her honeymoon wearing one. Instead of leaving her hair in the elaborate arrangement Mollie had worked on so diligently, she'd absently rebraided it in its usual style. Suddenly she felt embarrassed and out of place in these luxurious surroundings.

That laser gaze paused in its inspection of what he must consider her many shortcomings. She felt as though he was peering deep into her soul. "My son seems to have lost whatever manners he ever had," he said, his tone tinged with irony. He held out his hand. "As you've guessed, I'm his father. And you are—?"

Out of habit she used the name she'd had until a few hours ago. "Maribeth O'Brien..."

"Cochran," Chris smoothly added when she paused. "Maribeth and I were married earlier today."

Whatever his father's reaction to this news, Kenneth hid it well. His gaze veered to Chris. His voice, which he used with the skill of a musician playing an instrument, now carried a hint of amusement. "Really? I could have sworn you said you were attending a school chum's wedding. What happened? Did the bug suddenly bite you, as well?''

Maribeth couldn't believe this conversation. It was totally bizarre. It was as if the father was baiting his son about something as important as his marriage. She glanced at Chris to see his reaction, but like his father, Chris gave nothing of his thoughts away.

''Something like that'' was all he said. ''I'd like to take a few days off, if it's all right with you. Maybe Sam would be able to fill in for me on this trip, considering the circumstances.''

Kenneth continued to ignore Chris's request. ''Rather sudden, wasn't it?'' This time his intent gaze on her was deliberately provocative. She felt as though he was assessing everything about her, from the color and texture of her hair and the way she was dressed to the sandals on her feet. ''You two known each other long?''

Maribeth wasn't sure who he was talking to, but it didn't matter because Chris immediately answered, ''Long enough.'' His voice gave nothing of his thoughts or feelings away.

Kenneth laughed shortly and turned to the two men with him. ''I swear, the kid's becoming more like me every day.''

Maribeth almost shuddered. She couldn't think of anything worse. She was beginning to better understand his mother's comments. Kenneth Cochran was one of the most intimidating men she'd ever met. What must it have been like being married to him?

Kenneth turned back to them. ''Hell, Chris, you can honeymoon as well in Atlanta as you can in Dallas. Better, even. I'll put you up in the fanciest suite they've got there. Once we land, you won't need to do anything for me until we fly to Miami later in the week. What could be better?"

Maribeth could feel the tension emanating from Chris and wondered about it. She wasn't certain if he was angry or whether he didn't like having to be in a position to ask anything of his father.

She didn't want to cause trouble between the two men. "We could do that, couldn't we, Chris?" She smiled at Kenneth. "I've never been to Atlanta."

Once again Kenneth laughed. "Why doesn't that surprise me? From the looks of you, honey, I'd say you were freshly hatched." He winked at Chris. "You've got the right idea, son. Get 'em young and teach 'em yourself, right?"

A ripple moved through Chris and for a moment Maribeth was afraid he might lunge at the other man. He didn't. Instead he waited a moment before glancing at Maribeth. He smiled, but his eyes glittered with anger.

"In that case," Chris said, as though his father hadn't spoken, "We'll go to Atlanta tonight if you think you'd like that." He glanced around at the other men before his gaze rested on his father. "I'll need to get some clean clothes. I only took a few things with me when I packed earlier this week. I was counting on being able to repack before we left in the morning."

Kenneth reached into his inside breast pocket and pulled out a wallet. "No time for that. Here. You and your little missy can go shopping once we get to Atlanta." He handed what looked to be several hundred dollar bills to Chris. When he didn't reach out to take them, Kenneth calmly folded them and stuck them into Chris's shirt pocket. "Consider it the first of my wedding presents to you. I'm proud of you, son. You finally took a piece of my advice, may wonders never cease. I have to admit that you've surprised me. You've never shown much interest in being a dutiful son before." He glanced at Maribeth and winked. "I'm pleased you at least listened to me on this one. You've got a fine eye for quality, boy, I'll certainly give you that."

Kenneth turned to the other men. "Well, gentlemen. Find a place to get comfortable. You're in safe hands with Chris here flying us. He's the best there is, I've made damn sure of that!"

Chris took her hand. "C'mon. I'll show you around while I make sure everything's ready for this leg of the trip."

She was glad he didn't leave her in the plane with his father and friends. Things were happening faster than she could quite handle at the moment.

Maribeth slept most of the flight to Atlanta. Once she awakened, she kept her eyes closed rather than having to make conversation with Kenneth Cochran. Not that he paid her much attention once they were on their way. She dozed off with the sound of his voice filling the area around her. She couldn't make out much of the conversation, but it sounded as though he was persuading them to either invest with his company or to buy products he sold. He was quite a salesman, she would give him that. He wore his confidence and self-assurance as if it were a royal robe.

So this was Chris's father.

She'd learned more about Chris and his family today than in all the years they'd been friends. Thinking back, she realized that when they were children, she, Bobby and Chris rarely talked about their home life. She'd known that Chris lived with his mother during the school year and spent his summers in Dallas with his father.

Once he returned at the beginning of the new school year, the three of them took up where they'd left off when school was dismissed for the summer. Now that she thought about it, Chris had never talked about what it was like to live in Dallas, or what he did during those summers he was away. He just seemed eager to join in the group activities once he returned to Agua Verde.

Was that why he'd seemed such a loner? Had he made friends in Dallas? Had it been difficult to be pulled between the two parents? She didn't know because he never talked about himself.

He'd been a good student, much better than she was... or Bobby. Chris seemed to thrive on challenges back then.

Well, he'd certainly picked a new challenge to face now. Although she'd been planning for her marriage for most of her life, it now seemed Chris had never given it much thought.

Friendship was one thing. Marriage was a very different matter. She still didn't understand why he'd been willing to help her save face.

If she'd had more time to think it through, she wondered if she would have married him? At the time he'd offered her a short-range solution.

Only time would tell if a marriage between them would create more problems than it had solved.

Chris slipped the card into the slot of the hotel suite and opened the door, then turned and lifted her into his arms. "This wasn't exactly how I'd planned this, but I'm determined to carry you over the threshold," he said, his eyes smiling into hers.

"The bellhop's going to know we just got married," she whispered as she heard the elevator *ping* announcing that someone was getting off on this floor. At this late hour, it was a good guess that it was their luggage being delivered.

He stepped inside. "Who cares?" He spun her in a circle before allowing her to stand once more. "So, Mrs. Cochran. What do you think?"

She was still trying to take it all in when the bellhop brought in their luggage. He opened another set of double doors into a large bedroom area. She watched as he walked over and flipped on a light, then closed the draperies across the wide glass doors that went out onto a balcony.

"Does your father treat all his pilots this well?"

He laughed. "Hardly. He was showing off tonight. It doesn't matter who the audience is, he's immediately 'on.'"

"Does it bother you?" she asked, then waited while he tipped the bellhop and closed the door behind him.

"Does my father bother me? Sometimes. You'd think by now that I'd be used to him."

"How long have you worked for him?"

"About eight months."

"Oh! I thought— I just assumed that you went to work for him once we graduated."

"No. I never intended to work for him. It's ironic how things happen sometimes." He slowly paced back to where she stood in front of the bedroom doorway. "Are you hovering here in the doorway for a specific reason?"

"Uh, no, not really." She looked around uncertainly. "I'm not sure what to do next, that's all."

"Well, since it's after two o'clock local time, I don't think we'd be out of line to consider going to bed. What do you think?"

Although his tone was gentle, he made no effort to hide his amusement. She knew her face must be flaming but she refused to look away from him. "All right," she managed to say.

"Which suitcase do you want?"

"The smaller one."

He placed it on the rack. "There you are. I'll be a gentleman and let you have first use of the bathroom."

This was getting worse and worse. She felt so awkward. Was it like this for everyone? She wasn't used to sharing a room. She hadn't had to share a bathroom since Mollie got married. Why couldn't she feel more casual about all of this? After all, she was married. This was all perfectly normal. Or at least it would be once she got used to it.

She gathered up her gown and toiletry bag and hurried to the bathroom, closing the door behind her. Her image stared back in the mirror. Maribeth had never seen herself look so flustered and uncertain. She couldn't believe that she was acting so silly.

By the time she came out, she had changed into the white, tiny-pleated, full-length satin-and-lace nightgown Mollie had given her together with a matching robe. She concentrated on trying to feel relaxed and at ease with the situation. She was almost able to pull it off until she saw Chris.

He'd taken off his shirt, socks and shoes and was stretched out on the turned-back bed, his arms behind his head, watching her.

Maribeth felt as though she'd just received a body blow. Feeling winded, she could only stare at the wide expanse of muscled chest. He swung up and off the bed and when she would have stepped aside he stopped her with a touch. Leaning to kiss her, he said, "I'll be right back. Don't fall asleep on me."

She was still standing there when the bathroom door closed behind him. *Fat chance of that,* was all she could think of in response to his comment.

Hastily discarding her robe, she slid beneath the covers and fought the urge to drag them to her neck. Her gown adequately covered her. There was no reason to be embarrassed, she kept reminding herself.

The sound of the bathroom door opening made her jump before she could restrain herself. She glanced around and saw that Chris had removed his trousers. He was now wearing a pair of black briefs that clung to him as if they were a second skin.

She hastily averted her eyes, but couldn't seem to control the urge to glance back at him. He was gorgeous! Trim and lean and muscled, in obvious good physical condition.

As soon as he got into bed, she reached for the light the bellhop had turned on earlier.

"Would you mind if we leave the light on?" he asked.

"Uh, no. I, uh, just assumed that—"

He laughed. "Oh, I don't need a night-light, if that's what you're thinking. I'm just not quite ready to go to sleep. I want to see you . . . if that's all right with you."

She almost strangled herself trying to swallow. "Mmm," was the best she could manage as an answer.

"The bed's quite comfortable, don't you think?" he asked, smiling.

She nodded vigorously and made another strangled sound.

"Is the temperature all right for you? Would you rather have it warmer . . . or cooler?"

This time she vigorously shook her head. "It's fine," she said, sounding a little hoarse.

"Maribeth?" His voice was very soft.

"What?"

"You don't have to be afraid of me, you know. I'm not going to pounce on you."

"I realize that," she admitted. "I just don't know what to do."

"If you'd rather go on to sleep tonight, we can. I don't want you to feel pushed into anything—"

"Sleep! How can I possibly sleep? I've never slept with anybody in my whole life!"

He grinned. "Well, neither have I. It will be a new experience for both of us."

She stared at him with patent disbelief. "But you told me that— Well, I know you've had more experience than I have."

"Maybe," he conceded. "But probably not as much as you're imagining. And I've never actually slept with anyone. I've been looking forward to doing that with you, actually. Just the idea of sleeping with my arms around you is a fantasy I never thought to experience."

She relaxed a little, and slid back down beneath the covers. "You've fantasized about me?"

"Oh, yes. Many times . . . all kinds."

"Will you tell me about some of them?"

"I'd much rather show you," he said, and moved closer until he was lying close enough to touch her.

Five

She could feel the heat of his body radiating down her entire length and he hadn't as yet touched her. This man was potent stuff. She couldn't remember a time when she so desperately wanted to be relaxed and at ease. Instead she was so rattled, she couldn't think of anything to say or do in this situation.

Why hadn't she asked Megan or Mollie about what to expect? The truth was, none of them had ever discussed this aspect of marriage.

He placed his hand lightly on her stomach and she almost shot out of bed. "Try to relax," he murmured. "There's no rush, you know. I want you to feel comfortable."

She was feeling several different things at the moment, none of which came remotely close to comfortable. She took a deep breath and exhaled, a time-honored remedy to bring on a sense of relaxation.

Nope. It didn't work.

She was too aware of his hand. His thumb rested just beneath her breasts, while his fingers lay along the bottom of her rib cage. The silk covering her had never seemed so thin. She could almost feel the material heating. It would be a wonder if there weren't scorch marks soon.

She swallowed, hard.

"What would you like to do?" he asked.

"Do?" she croaked.

"Have you any fantasies you'd like to check out?"

Despite what she'd expected, she was beginning to adjust to his warm hand resting against her. He was propped up on his other elbow, his expression very tender.

Hesitantly she touched the curls on his chest with her fingers. He made a soft noise that sounded suspiciously like a purr.

"You like that?"

"Yes, ma'am, I certainly do. You have my permission to touch me as much as you'd like."

Maribeth was pleased with the idea of being the one touching, of being in control. She shifted so that she could face him. His hand quite naturally continued to move around her waist and rested lightly on her hip. He allowed his fingers to drift lazily back and forth, sliding the silken material over her skin. She liked the feel of that as well.

She brushed her fingers across his chest, feeling the smooth surface covering the muscled expanse. When she touched his nipples hidden in the mat of curls, he took a quick breath. She could feel his heartbeat increase.

A sense of power swept over her, one she'd never felt before. She forgot to feel nervous in pursuit of this new pleasure she'd discovered.

He sighed and relaxed back against the pillow. She traced the shape of his brows and nose, his cheek and jaw, and the sensuous curve of his upper lip. He made that purring sound again.

Acting on impulse she placed her lips over his. They were as warm as she remembered and quickly responded to the light pressure. He wrapped his arms around her and took over the kiss.

By the time he pulled away slightly, they were both breathless. In addition, Maribeth knew exactly how she affected him. He was holding her pressed tightly against him so that there was no doubt.

He slipped one of the straps off her shoulder and lingeringly stroked a line from her ear down to the top of her breast. Her nipple hardened in response. As though to appease it, he rubbed his thumb across the pebbled nub in a soothing gesture that didn't do a thing to soothe her.

She shifted restlessly, feeling warm and wanting. What, she wasn't sure, but she knew that he was stirring something inside her.

He kissed her again, this time leaning over her, his chest rubbing against her sensitive breasts. As though her hands understood what she wanted better than she did at the moment, they stroked his back from shoulders to buttocks. His briefs now seemed to be an unnecessary barrier. She slipped her hands under the thin cotton material and squeezed the taut muscles beneath.

"Do you want them off?" he whispered, suddenly breaking the kiss.

"Mmm-hmm."

"Then take them off."

She immediately responded to his suggestion by sliding his briefs down as far as she could reach. He lifted and she reached around to pull the front down and found a whole new world to explore.

Chris helped her by shoving the offending garment down his legs and off his feet. Maribeth was already otherwise occupied exploring what she had found. She forgot her shyness in discovering how each touch affected him so strongly.

She'd had no idea that a man's body could feel this way. She'd never seen a man nude, but wasn't ignorant of the male shape and form. However, a tactile exploration revealed additional information—the smoothness, the sensitivity, and the involuntary movement of his hips as he surged into her hands when she lightly moved her fingertips from base to tip.

She gazed into his eyes, caught up in a delicious sense of awe. "I had no idea," she whispered.

"What?"

"I don't know, exactly. How wonderful it feels just to touch you, to hold you, to have you trust me, to experience your response. All of it. I had no idea that lovemaking could feel this good."

Her candid explanation must have pleased him because he kissed her again. This time his tongue kept the same pace as his hips as he moved against her. When he slipped the other strap off her shoulder she felt his bare skin brush against her newly uncovered breasts.

He raised his head and she was startled to see the look on his face. There was nothing impassive about him now. His eyes glittered and his face was flushed. She felt a surge of pleasure sweep over her at the sight. He was no longer the aloof loner he appeared to be with others. At least not here. Not now.

He lowered his head once again, his lips encircling the tip of her breast. When he gently tugged, ever-new sensations swept over her and she almost cried out with the feeling. She ran her hands through his thick hair, holding him to her, silently encouraging him.

He moved to her other breast, alternating his movements of slightly tugging, then soothing them with his tongue. Maribeth surprised herself with her own reaction. She lifted her hips slightly, her excitement accelerating when Chris met her movements with ones of his own. The feel of him pressed so wonderfully close to her filled her with such an intensity of emotion that she wasn't sure she could handle it.

"Oh, Chris," she whispered, her breathing broken. "Oh, Chris" was all she could think of to say.

When he slipped his hand beneath her gown and trailed it lingeringly up to the top of her thighs, she shivered and almost cried out. She didn't know her own body anymore while he seemed to know exactly what to do to elicit an ever-stronger response from deep within her.

He touched her where no one had ever touched her before. Instead of feeling embarrassed or shy, she welcomed him, lifting to the palm of his hand, where it massaged across her tight curls in a circular motion.

When his fingers explored further, she opened to him, breathlessly begging him to help her deal with what was happening to her. She felt as though she were being wound tighter and tighter inside.

"It's okay, honey. You're doing fine...oh, so fine," he whispered, his breathing not much better than hers.

He lifted the gown so that he could rest his lower body between her thighs. Oh, yes. That was what she'd wanted. She reached for him and he immediately took her hand and held it beside her head.

"Not now, honey, or it'll be all over." There was a rueful chuckle in his words.

He felt even bigger than she'd expected, but she didn't care. She wanted him closer. She wanted him inside her. With frustration fanned by untutored desire, she raised her hips, forcing him closer. Her move, together with his own, more careful motion thrust him into her.

She felt the discomfort but didn't care. Instead she wrapped her arms and legs around him, silently pleading for she knew not what.

He knew what she wanted. Even so, he held himself motionless, gazing down at her with a mixture of amazement and need. She was so beautiful, and he'd wanted her for so long. Now that she was actually his, he wanted her to share what he was feeling, now that he was finally with her.

He concentrated on pacing himself, while he continued to stimulate her. She came apart in his arms, her soft cry triggering his own release. All he could do was hold on.

The next thing he was aware of were the muscles quivering in his arms and legs due to the effort of keeping his full weight off her. Sighing, he lowered himself to the bed, holding her tightly against him.

Only then did it occur to him that he'd never bothered to completely remove her gown. It was bunched around her waist. When he could find enough air to speak, he said, "Your beautiful gown may never be the same."

She still held on to him, her face buried against his neck. She muttered something.

"What?"

She raised her head, her eyes shining. "It was worth it."

Damn! But she was beautiful. Her fiery curls trailed across her shoulders and over her breast. He ran his fingers through the silken mass, finding that even that took almost more energy than he had at the moment.

"That was more than I could have possibly fantasized," she admitted after a long silence. "I feel so strange, as though I've turned into somebody else."

He continued to play with her hair. "There was nothing wrong with the other one."

"I didn't know my body could feel so—I don't know— tingly and achy. It was like you started building some kind of fire deep inside of me that took over."

"I didn't want to scare you by moving too fast." He closed his eyes. "I was worried that I would disappoint you."

She shook her head. "Never."

After another few minutes he was able to get out of bed. He went into the bathroom and after a moment returned with a warm, damp washcloth. Slipping into bed once again he slowly and carefully touched her. This time she was very aware of what he was doing and her cheeks glowed.

"Thank you," she whispered.

"It's my pleasure." His gaze caught hers and they laughed together, their voices soft and intimate. After returning the cloth to the bathroom, he helped her with her gown. "Off or on."

"Would it be brazen to admit I'd like to sleep all night with our skin touching?"

"Not brazen at all. However, I have to tell you that we may be able to fall asleep that way, but I can bet you any amount of money I'll be aware of you all night."

"Oh, well, if it bothers you—"

"Oh, it will. I'm looking forward to it." He pulled her into the curl of his body, her back against his chest. "How's that?"

"Wonderful," she said, sounding sleepy.

He smiled to himself and closed his eyes. That was as good a word as any to describe it.

Maribeth lay there, listening to Chris's breathing even out into deep sleep. She wished she could do the same. Everything was too different for her to relax.

Her mind was filled with racing thoughts, none of which she seemed able to control.

This was her wedding night. She'd just spent an incredible time with Chris. Now she lay next to him, his arm across her waist, in a totally new environment to what she was used to.

She'd wanted to leave home and grow up. Meeting Kenneth Cochran had been one of many shocks she'd received today.

Why hadn't she realized that Chris came from a wealthy background? Was it because they each had been raised on a ranch, not known as a get-rich occupation? She couldn't recall that he had dressed differently from other schoolmates. There had been no indication to give her a clue.

So she looked as though she'd just hatched, did she? She didn't care what Kenneth Cochran thought about her, but she didn't like the idea that he was using her to put Chris in an indefensible place.

She'd never bothered with fashion or the latest styles. But she could. She was intelligent, educated and knew she could hold her own with anyone.

Chris shifted slightly, momentarily tightening his hold around her. Even asleep, he made certain she was there beside him.

It was also time for her to take a good, hard look at what she had done—and what she had admitted—by marrying Chris.

Bobby's actions had been inexcusable and she had been justifiably hurt. However, if she had been truly heartbroken, she could not have married Chris. She wasn't going to kid herself about that.

She had never felt toward Bobby what Chris had caused her to feel tonight. She'd never been tempted to explore this side of her nature before. And yet she had wanted Chris to make love to her. She'd wanted to know what it was all about.

What was it about Chris that made him so different from everyone else she'd known?

She wasn't certain she knew what it was, but it called to her in ways she didn't understand.

She yawned, enjoying the warmth of his chest and legs behind her. Her last waking thought was wondering if Bobby had discovered all these new feelings with someone else. If so, she could better understand his behavior.

A sliver of light across her eyelids woke her several hours later. Maribeth forced her eyes open and stared at the closed draperies that didn't quite meet in the middle. She was too comfortable to get out of bed and adjust them, so she turned away, burrowing her head into the pillow.

Except this particular pillow was a great deal more firm and was breathing. That was enough to bring her fully awake.

Chris lay asleep beside her. The light didn't touch him. She propped herself up on her elbows and stared at him, enjoying looking at this man she'd married.

He had impossibly long, thick lashes. His skin was tanned, as though he spent time working out in the sun. His thick, black hair tumbled over his forehead, looking boyish.

Chris never looked boyish, even when he'd been one. He'd always acted so much older than the rest of them. Perhaps it had been his expression more than anything.

The sudden ringing of the phone made her leap. Even more surprising was Chris's immediate reaction. He was reaching for the phone on his side of the bed before it finished the first ring, his eyes already open. He'd gone from sound sleep to awake in a heartbeat.

"Cochran," he muttered into the phone.

That was all he said for the longest time. He'd rolled away from her so she was watching his back and saw the muscles tense as he continued to listen.

"Is there a possibility he could be mistaken?"

Once again there was a long silence while he listened.

"I understand" was his final comment before hanging up the phone. With his back still to her, Chris sat up on the side of the bed and propped his elbows on his thighs. He dropped his head into his hands.

"Bad news?"

Slowly he straightened and looked around at her. His dark eyes looked bleak. "I'm sorry. Did the phone wake you?"

His voice sounded flat. Maribeth was suddenly aware of her lack of clothing. She tugged the sheet a little higher on her chest. "No. I was watching you sleep."

That elicited a half smile from him. "That sounds boring. You should have awakened me." He stretched

PLAY
ONE MILLION
BIG BUCKS
ONE MILLION
AND YOU COULD WIN THE
$1,000,000.00
PLUS JACKPOT!
YOUR PERSONAL GAME CARD INSIDE...
SILHOUETTE

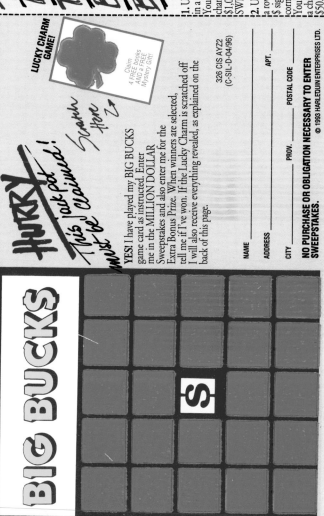

BIG BUCKS

$

TWO WAYS TO WIN BIG BUCKS!

1. Uncover 5 $ signs in a row...BINGO! You're eligible for a chance to win the $1,000,000.00 SWEEPSTAKES!

2. Uncover 5 $ signs in a row AND uncover $ signs in all 4 corners...BINGO! You're also eligible for a chance to win the $50,000.00 EXTRA BONUS PRIZE!

HURRY! This Jackpot must be claimed!

Scratch Here →

LUCKY CHARM GAME!

Claim 4 FREE books AND a FREE Mystery Gift!

YES! I have played my BIG BUCKS game card as instructed. Enter me in the MILLION DOLLAR Sweepstakes and also enter me for the Extra Bonus Prize. When winners are selected, tell me if I've won. If the Lucky Charm is scratched off I will also receive everything revealed, as explained on the back of this page.

326 CIS AYZ2
(C-SIL-D-04/96)

NAME _____

ADDRESS _____ APT. _____

CITY _____ PROV. _____ POSTAL CODE _____

THE SILHOUETTE READER SERVICE™: HERE'S HOW IT WORKS

Accepting free books places you under no obligation to buy anything. You may keep the books and gift and return the shipping statement marked "cancel". If you do not cancel, about a month later we will send you 6 additional novels and bill you just $2.99 each plus 25¢ delivery and GST*. That's the complete price, and – compared to cover prices of $3.99 each – quite a bargain! You may cancel at any time, but if you choose to continue, every month we'll send you 6 more books, which you may either purchase at the discount price...or return at our expense and cancel your subscription.

*Terms and prices subject to change without notice. Canadian residents add applicable provincial taxes and GST.

019561919-L2A5X3-BR01

SILHOUETTE READER SERVICE
PO BOX 609
FORT ERIE ON L2A 9Z9

MAIL ≥ POSTE
Canada Post Corporation / Société canadienne des postes
Postage paid   Port payé
if mailed in Canada   si posté au Canada

Business   **Réponse**
Reply   **d'affaires**

019561919   01

complete and mail your Official Entry Form. If your Official Entry Form is missing, or you wish to obtain an additional ent...

out beside her once again, the sheet haphazardly drawn across his loins. "Good morning, Mrs. Cochran," he murmured, kissing her lightly. "Did you sleep well?"

He was saying all the right things, but there was something wrong. It showed in his eyes. "Fine."

"Do you think you can get used to sharing a bed with me?"

There. She could see more life, more heat in his gaze now. "I think so," she replied absently. "Is something wrong?"

His eyes narrowed. "What do you mean?"

"The phone call."

"Oh. Work related."

"I thought your father wasn't going to need you for the next few days."

There was a long pause, as though he was searching for a reply. When it came, it didn't seem to have anything to do with their conversation. "I wasn't thinking very clearly this past week or I would have realized that this wasn't an ideal time to get married."

She froze. "I see."

"It has nothing to do with you. It's just that—" He paused, obviously searching for words. "My life's a little complicated at the moment."

"You forgot it was complicated?" she carefully repeated.

"I tend to forget a lot of things when I'm around you," he admitted, sliding his hand along her arm to her shoulder, then allowing it to slip down to her breast. His breathing changed, and his expression was suddenly filled with longing.

"Chris? What is it?"

He turned to her fully, his thigh finding the space between her legs and claiming it. "Honey, I would tell you about it if I could. But I can't. Not now, at any rate. There was nothing unusual planned for this trip. I saw no reason not to bring you along. And now—" He sighed. "It looks like I may be busier than I thought."

She almost laughed with the relief she felt. "Is that all? Oh, Chris, I don't mind. If you need to go somewhere, don't worry about me. I can entertain myself. I'm not helpless, you know."

He nibbled on her earlobe, causing shivers to run up and down her body. "I don't want to leave you for a minute. I finally have you exactly where I want you...in my bed."

"You're going to find me in your bed. Never fear."

Then there were no other words. Chris made love to her almost desperately, holding her, whispering hot words of passion, making her quiver with her own need. The gentle lover of the night before was gone. In his place was an erotic, passionate man who sent her spinning into orbit.

She clung to him, too overwhelmed with feeling to do more than hang on while he guided them both into ever-expanding sensuous pleasure.

When he collapsed on the bed beside her, she was too limp to do more than slide her fingers across his moist chest.

They lay there together, the only sound in the room their harsh breathing. When he could find his breath, he said, "I'm sorry. I didn't mean to hurt you."

"You didn't."

He rolled out of the bed and strode to the bathroom, pausing at the door. "I'm going to have to go out for a while. I'll leave you some money. Maybe you'd like to look around, see a movie or something."

"Okay."

"I'm sorry. It's a hell of a thing to do to you the first day of our honeymoon."

She was having a little trouble concentrating on his words while he stood there so unconcernedly naked. Her gaze kept darting over his long, lean frame, pausing to admire the way he was put together. "I'll be all right. Really."

In a few quick strides he returned to the bed and scooped her up. "Let's shower together. That should save some time."

Unfortunately for whoever might be waiting on Chris, a shared shower did nothing to shorten his leaving the suite.

Six

Maribeth was fascinated by the types of stores in the
mall not far from their hotel. She'd eaten a salad in the
hotel coffee shop before venturing out.

When she got a glimpse of herself in one of the shop
windows, she couldn't believe there were no outward
changes to reflect how differently she felt inside.

Chris had made her feel like the most beautiful woman
in the world. And the sexiest. However, the plait and
simple dress she wore still spoke of the country. She
wanted to change that. She wanted to look her very best
when Chris returned to the hotel.

She spotted a store that had several attractive outfits in
the window. Once inside, a salesperson appeared, offering assistance. Maribeth candidly explained what she was
hoping to do and the woman agreed to help her.

Two hours later she walked out with several bags and
the telephone number of a salon that offered, in addi-

tion to hairstyles and makeovers, such things as manicures and massages.

She returned to the hotel and put all her purchases away, then called and made an appointment at the salon.

Instead of attending a movie, she spent several hours having her hair shaped, shortened and layered, having a full body massage, a pedicure and manicure.

After that, she shopped for shoes.

By the time she reached the hotel, she'd learned things about herself that she'd never known before.

The woman who'd helped her select clothes complimented her model-slender shape. The man at the salon rhapsodized over the color and texture of her hair. The woman who gave her tips on makeup couldn't say enough about the unusual color and shape of her eyes, her sparkling smile, her flawless complexion.

None of those things made any difference to her, but Maribeth was pleased that she wouldn't be an embarrassment to Chris. By the time she slipped into one of the dressier outfits she'd bought, there was no sign in the mirror of the country girl Chris had married.

She postponed eating dinner, choosing to wait in the comfortable suite until Chris returned.

Chris glanced at his watch once he stepped into the elevator and frowned. He'd been gone much longer than he'd wanted to be or intended to be. The series of meetings he'd attended hadn't put him in the best of moods. It didn't help any that those attending the meeting had already heard of his sudden and unexpected marriage. He'd had to listen to a bunch of sophomoric comments from several of them, and a chastisement from his supervisor about the poor timing.

Well, how was he to know that all hell was going to break loose during his honeymoon, for God's sake? He'd been a part of this operation for two years. He'd managed to wring a very grudging permission from his supervisor that afternoon to share some of what he was doing with Maribeth. Not much, but enough so that she would understand his periodic disappearances.

He opened the door to their suite and saw Maribeth sitting on the sofa reading. His breath caught in his throat. What had she done to herself?

She glanced up at the sound of the door opening. By the time he'd shut the door, she'd tossed her book aside and stood.

"Hi. I hope you haven't eaten. I waited for you."

"I haven't eaten...what have you done? Where did you find that dress? Your hair...you've cut your hair." He couldn't seem to take in the transformation from the young woman he'd left this morning to the sophisticate standing before him.

She chuckled and turned in a circle. "What do you think? Do you like it?"

Her hair now fell in waves around her face and shoulders. The dress she wore clung to her figure, the color bringing out the golden topaz hue of her eyes.

He had trouble concentrating on her eyes.

The dress emphasized her full breasts, slender waist and curving hips. It also showed off a considerable length of her legs.

"Like it?" He cleared his throat. "You look, uh, different. That is, very glamorous. You—"

"You don't like it, do you?" she asked, coming closer. "I'll admit it takes some getting used to."

Her eyes looked larger. They sparkled with a mysterious glow. He touched her hair. It still felt silky and so soft. Standing this close to her was having a predictable effect on him.

"They really didn't cut all that much off of it, except around my face."

"You look stunning, Maribeth. I'm not sure how I'm going to handle the reaction you're going to cause when we go downstairs."

"I don't understand. Who's downstairs?"

He grinned. "The entire male population. You're going to start a stampede . . . at the very least have them drooling."

She kissed him. "I thought you were being serious."

"I am very serious." He slid his hands over her hips and rested them in the small of her back. "Are you wearing any underwear?"

"Of course." She moved as though she intended to show him. He stopped her hand.

"If you intend to have dinner anytime soon, you'll get out of arm's reach of me and give me a chance to change clothes."

She obediently—much to his disappointment—stepped back and waved to the bedroom. "I'll wait here."

"Good idea," he growled, striding into the other room. His reaction to her had caught him off guard. It wasn't as if he hadn't made love to her several times in the past twenty-four hours. He certainly wasn't love-starved, but he was acting like it. If he didn't watch it, he'd be howling at the moon any moment now.

By the time he changed into one of his suits, he was in better shape to be seen in public. The hotel had a very nice restaurant on the top floor. He called to reserve a table, then returned to the other room. "Ready?"

"Oh, my. You look sensational."

"You're just not used to seeing me in a suit."

"That's true." He opened the door for her and she stepped out into the hallway. "I thought you looked smashing in the tux, but this isn't bad. Not bad at all."

He took her hand on the way to the elevator. "Don't say I didn't warn you," he said, pushing the Up button.

"About what?"

"That dress."

"Is it that conspicuous?"

"No. It's what you look like in it."

The elevator let them off in the foyer of the restaurant. Chris gave the maître d' his name, and they were immediately led to a table for two by one of the large windows looking out over Atlanta. The city sparkled with lights.

"This is wonderful, Chris."

The table had a single rosebud in a vase as well as a candle glowing. Maribeth was having trouble taking it all in. "Have you been here before?" she asked.

"Yes. My father prefers staying here when he's in town."

"Speaking of your father, did you remind him that he promised not to disturb us until it's time to fly to Miami?"

So. There it was. The opening he needed to tell her.

Just then the waiter arrived with the menus. "Are you hungry for anything in particular?" Chris asked.

"Anything's fine."

"Would you like me to order for you?"

"Please."

It was strange, the things he knew about her. He remembered her favorite foods, as well as those things she didn't like, so that it was easy enough to glance through the menu and choose their meals.

Once alone, he said, "There's something I need to tell you."

"It sounds serious."

"It's about today. My business had nothing to do with my father."

"I'm afraid I don't understand."

"Remember I told you I never intended to work for my father?"

"Yes."

"For the past three and a half years I've been working for an agency of the government that's working to prevent drug trafficking across our borders. My pilot license has come in handy on numerous occasions, but it also created the situation I'm in now."

She was looking at him as though she'd never seen him before. "You're a government agent?"

"Yeah."

"Like a spy?"

He shrugged. "Sometimes. It depends on the operation."

"Then your father—"

"That's what I need to tell you. My father knows nothing about my government work. When my supervisor found out that my father wanted me to work for him, in any capacity, I was assigned the job."

"Meaning you weren't given a choice."

"That's right. My supervisor felt it was too good a cover for me to pass up." The waiter appeared with their wine. After signaling that it was acceptable, Chris waited until they each had a glass. He touched his glass to hers. "To us."

She took a sip, her mind obviously on their previous conversation. "Why couldn't you tell your father about your other job?"

"Because he might not have taken me on, otherwise. My supervisor didn't want to take a chance on blowing the cover."

"You mean he's never known what you did for a living?"

"No. I have as little to do with my father and his life-style as possible, even though he still insists that he intends to turn his empire over to me someday."

She stared at him in disbelief. "You mean you don't want it?"

"Not if it means working for him on a permanent basis. The less I have to do with him, the better I like it."

"Is he a part of the investigation you're presently working on?"

Silence stretched between them. He reached for his wineglass and took a sip before he spoke again. "What makes you ask that?"

Now she felt uncomfortable. Was she treading into areas that were none of her business? Surely Chris would say something to that effect. Deciding to take his question at face value she said, "I'm not sure, actually. Just little things. Mostly the way you are around your father. You don't act as though you like him very much. That attitude may go back to something that happened in your childhood, but somehow, I feel it's more than that. I get the feeling that you don't like him very much as a man, not just as a father."

He looked at her for a long time before saying, "You're very astute."

"And you haven't answered my question."

He leaned back in his chair and casually glanced around the restaurant. "I really can't discuss any more of this. I'm sorry. The reason I'm telling you anything at all is because some things are suddenly heating up in this particular operation and, like it or not, I'll be spending most of this week in meetings. For the record, I don't like it and I've lodged my complaint with the powers that be, for all the good it does me. They seem to find it amusing that I'm not going to be able to spend much time with my bride on our honeymoon. As far as my father is concerned, though, that's exactly what I'll be doing... lazing around."

"Is that what he thought you were doing before you went to work for him, lazing around?"

His smile was brief but amused. "Something like that, yeah."

"I get the impression you enjoy doing things that your father disapproves of."

"I don't care what his opinion of me is."

The waiter arrived with their salads. They began to eat in silence. When Chris appeared to have dropped their conversation Maribeth finally asked, "Could you actually use evidence you uncover while you're working for him to build a case against your father?"

"Maribeth. I told you, I can't discuss that aspect of the investigation... not with you or anyone else. I'm just doing my job, doing what I'm told to do. Whatever happens, happens."

She touched his hand lying on the table. "Oh, Chris. You can't make me believe that you don't care what happens to him. He's your father, no matter what ill will is between you. Whether you'll admit it or not, this must be terribly painful for you."

He looked down at her hand, then turned his over so that he could hold hers. "I can deal with it, Maribeth. I've been dealing with it for several months, now. It's just that, now that we're married, you need to know the truth about what I do."

"This is what you meant this morning, wasn't it, about the timing of our marriage?"

"Yeah. It would have been much wiser for me to have postponed getting married until all of this was tied up. To be honest, from the time Bobby called me, I never gave my job a thought. All I was thinking about was what you were going through."

"I'm sorry. If I'd known, I probably—"

"I'm not sorry in the least and I'm glad you made the decision you did. We'll get through this. It won't be much longer from the looks of things."

Their dinners arrived. This time neither one of them went back to the conversation, although Maribeth could think of little else.

She felt as though she'd stepped into another dimension. Chris a government agent? That was the last thing she'd been expecting to hear from him.

Her new husband was definitely full of surprises.

Kenneth Cochran was alone when they met him at the plane on Thursday.

"My God!" he said, taking off his sunglasses to look at Maribeth. "You look stunning, woman. Marriage obviously agrees with you."

"Thank you," she said, secretly pleased that she'd been able to make such an impression on him. She was finding that she rather enjoyed creating a stir, such as the one in the lobby when they'd checked out this morning. Chris had been amused that she'd been caught off guard by the looks she'd gotten.

"I warned you, didn't I?" he'd teased, helping her into the cab later.

That teasing man was nowhere in sight at the moment. She noted that the two men didn't bother to exchange greetings when they met.

"I guess I don't have to ask if you enjoyed your stay in Atlanta," Kenneth said. "You're positively glowing."

She glanced at Chris from the corner of her eye. "I enjoyed it very much."

Once on board, Kenneth waved to the seat where she'd sat before, then took the one beside her when Chris went to the cockpit. Kenneth reached for her hand. "I'm glad to hear you enjoyed Atlanta," he said, giving her hand a squeeze. "I want the two of you to be happy. The room was all right?"

"The suite was extraordinary. Thank you for your generous gift."

He patted her hand, then let go of it. "That's just the beginning, my dear. You'd be a very easy lady to spoil, I must say. I never thought I'd ever find myself envying my son, but I'm coming very close to it."

His tone was teasing and she tried to take his comments that way. However, she used the need to fasten her seat belt to ease away from him.

"Have you ever been to Miami before?"

"No. As you pointed out when we met, I'm really just a country girl."

"Now, I didn't mean anything by that. I was just teasing Chris a little. He's always so blasted secretive about his personal life. Why, Bambi and I have the hardest time getting him to come over to the house to visit. I practically have to commandeer him to attend our parties. The rest of the time we never hear from him."

"Bambi?"

His smile was dazzling. "My wife. Now there is one luscious lady. You're going to enjoy getting to know her,

I'm sure. She's a character. Great sense of humor, loves to have fun. Now that you're part of the family, maybe Chris will be a little more sociable.''

Maribeth was thankful the flight was no longer than it was. Once they leveled off, she excused herself to use the bathroom, then deliberately lingered in there. When she came out, Kenneth had moved to a table where he'd spread papers to work on, explaining that he'd be able to chat with her once he checked on a few things. However, they were already approaching Miami before he finished.

She was so relieved to see Chris when he finally stepped out of the cockpit that she wanted to throw her arms around his neck.

"When do you want to return to Dallas?" he asked Kenneth once they were through at the hangar where they'd left the plane.

"I should be through by noon on Saturday. I'd stay over the weekend except Bambi has this big party planned for that night, which the two of you are expected to attend, by the way. Bambi can hardly wait to meet Maribeth.''

Chris ignored the mention of a party. "We'll meet you here at one o'clock on Saturday, all right?" Chris took Maribeth's hand and led her from the hangar, leaving Kenneth standing there. "We'll get a cab to the hotel," he told her, "and get checked in, then we can spend some time on the beach."

She clung to him, glad to be with him again. She didn't know how to hide her nervousness around his father, even though he'd never been less than charming to her. Now she could relax, knowing she would have Chris to herself for a few days.

She'd seen very little of him during the days they'd been in Atlanta, but their nights had more than made up for any feelings of neglect she might have harbored.

And now...here they were in Miami. He promised her that morning not to leave her side for the next forty-eight hours. She was already planning on new ways to keep him entertained. She wasn't looking forward to their return to Dallas. Dallas would force her to face the reality of their lives. She would see his home—the place where they would be living. She might also discover that she was hopeless as the proper mate for Chris.

But for now, she refused to look ahead. This was her honeymoon and she intended to create all kinds of memories to look back upon.

"Where will your dad be staying?" she asked when Chris gave the taxi driver the name of the hotel he wanted.

"He has a condo down here."

"Have you ever stayed there?"

"A few times, but I prefer to have my own place."

She leaned back in the seat, looking out the window. "You know, Chris, I can't help feeling sad that you and your father don't get along better."

He sighed, causing her to look around at him. She'd never seen his expression quite so pensive. "I learned at an early age that my parents saw me as an object to fight over, a way to hurt each other in their power struggle. My father was determined to punish my mother. He never forgave her for walking out on him."

"She seems to be holding a great deal of resentment against him, even now, if her attitude at the wedding was any indication."

"I know, but there's nothing I can do about it. There's nothing sadder than people who refuse to let go of the past. They miss so much in life that's happening at the moment." He glanced over at her and grinned. "Take right now, as an example. Here we are talking about things that have already happened, over which we have absolutely no control, instead of discussing how we intend to spend the day. Any ideas about what you'd like to see while you're here?"

"Not really. I assumed you had something in mind."

He gave her a lingering kiss. When he eased away from her she was trembling. He had a way of reducing her bones to molten lava. "What I have in mind won't do much for you in the way of sight-seeing," he whispered, nuzzling her ear.

"Well, we can, uh, check into the hotel, maybe get something to eat, then wait until it's a little cooler to walk on the beach. How does that sound?"

"Fine with me. However, that leaves us with several hours unaccounted for."

She glanced at the back of the driver's head before glancing back at Chris with a grin. "I suppose we can always improvise."

Chris laughed, kissing her again. "An excellent idea."

And an excellent time they had, too!

When they arrived in Dallas the following Saturday the first thing Maribeth saw when she stepped off the plane was Chris's red car parked by the hangar. It was the most familiar thing she knew in the week since she married him.

They were finally home and ready to begin their life together.

His father stopped them on their way to the car. "Don't forget tonight, Chris. I want to introduce Maribeth to all my friends and associates. You don't have to stay long, of course. After all, you're newlyweds, but I expect you to put in an appearance."

Chris glanced at Maribeth before saying, "I'll let you know."

"That's not good enough. I want your word that you'll be there."

Maribeth could see that Chris was uncomfortable. She squeezed his hand. "I'm sure we can drop by for a while."

Without looking at her, Chris said to his father, "All right."

Kenneth slapped him on the shoulder. "You might surprise yourself and find that you actually enjoy it. I know Bambi will be thrilled to see you. I talked to her last night. She can hardly wait to meet Maribeth."

Chris said nothing more when they got into the car. Maribeth could feel her excitement mount now that they were actually driving toward her new home.

"Tell me about your house," she said. "You mentioned that you bought one. Isn't that a little unusual, being single?"

"I suppose, but I was never one who enjoyed apartment or condominium living. I lived on the ranch too long to feel comfortable close to other people. I happened to hear about this place through a mutual friend. The couple who owned it were divorcing and wanted a quick sale. I offered them what they wanted without having to go through a Realtor so it worked out well for all of us."

"How large is it?"

"The house is comfortable, about three thousand square feet. Plus, there's a little acreage that went with it, which is nice. I have room for a couple of horses and don't have to deal with close neighbors."

"It sounds wonderful. I wasn't certain what to expect."

They headed north from the Addison airport and were soon into rolling hills with fewer signs of the city. Chris drove with smooth efficiency, following the winding road and making the necessary turns. When he finally slowed, she saw a stone pillar with a mailbox and the name Cochran.

They had arrived. She couldn't control the excitement that seemed to grow within her.

He turned into the driveway and followed the lane up to the house and around it to a three-car garage in back. Hitting the remote, he waited for the door to open, then pulled the car inside.

Turning off the key, Chris turned to her and said, "Welcome to your new home, Mrs. Cochran." He got out of the car and walked around to the other side, opening her door. She took his proffered hand and got out.

He smoothed his hands over her arms, then turned away to unload her bags from the trunk. "C'mon. Let me show you the place," he said, gathering their luggage. He opened the connecting door between the garage and the house and motioned for her to enter first.

Chris led her from the back of the house to a curving staircase in the front foyer. Her eyes grew larger with every step.

By the time they walked the length of the upstairs hallway she knew that once again she'd underestimated the life she had chosen.

He set the bags in the middle of a large bedroom. "This will be our room." He nodded toward one wall. "I thought the stone fireplace a nice touch for the bedroom and the view is great from here."

Maribeth paused in the middle of the room, trying to take it all in.

"Come look at the bathroom. They overdid it a little, but I have to admit it's great to crawl into the spa tub and let those water jets wash the aches away."

She walked across the bedroom and peeked inside the doorway to the smaller room. The large Jacuzzi tub could easily hold three people and the freestanding glass shower an equal number. Two walls were mirrored from floor to ceiling and the floor was covered with the same plush carpeting that covered the entire upstairs.

"I didn't realize—" she mumbled, then stopped. She turned away and began to study the bedroom.

"You didn't realize what?"

"When you described the house, I guess I pictured something like the ranch house that had been around for generations. But this . . . this is so much newer and obviously more expensive."

He stayed where he was in the doorway of the bathroom and watched as she trailed her fingers over several pieces of furniture, pausing to look with concentrated interest at the pictures hanging on the walls.

Sometimes she was so easy to read. He wasn't sure how to handle this. Didn't she understand that it was her lack of interest in the amount of money he might have that had always endeared her to him?

"Does it bother you?" he finally asked when it became obvious that she wasn't going to say anything more.

She didn't answer right away. Finally she turned and faced him, the width of the room between them. "A little, I guess. I feel stupid not to have known. I should have understood, I mean—" she shrugged "—that car you drive is probably terribly expensive. At least I've never seen one like it before. Now I understand why Deke was

going on about it. You must have found it funny that I
was comparing it to a pickup truck.''

"Not funny in the way you mean. I wasn't laughing at
you, or making fun of you because you didn't know. You
gave me your candid response to it. That's one of the
reasons I appreciate you. You say exactly what you think
and feel. There's no pretense about you at all. I like
that.''

"I don't really fit with a place like this. I'd be scared
to drive your car. And as far as this house…'' She shook
her head, unable to find the words to describe what she
was feeling.

Chris walked over and took both of her hands. "I
don't want you to ever feel that you don't fit into my life.
We go back a long way together. I'm still the same guy.
Nothing's really changed.''

He put his arms around her. "I was able to buy this
house because of some money my dad's parents left me,
that's all. I decided that investing it in real estate was as
good as having it drawing interest somewhere.''

She rested her head on his shoulder. Maribeth wasn't
sure how long they stood there before she noticed the
light on his answering machine was blinking. She reluctantly pulled away from him. "It looks like you have
some messages waiting for you.''

He glanced over at them. "Nothing urgent, I'm sure.''

"If you'd like to check them, go ahead. I think I'm
going to take a shower.'' She forced herself to smile. "I
hope I don't get lost in there.''

She was already in the bathroom with the door closed
when she heard him play his machine messages back.
Three were men discussing upcoming meetings. One was
a female with a very sultry voice. "I wish you'd return my
calls, Chris, honey. This is the third message I've left.

You can't have been out of town all the time. It's really important that I speak to you no later than Saturday, the tenth. Please call me.''

The heat in the voice was enough to curl her hair. Today was the tenth. She wondered how long the message had been on there. Maybe it had been waiting for him to return from Agua Verde.

Maribeth quickly turned on the shower, to drown out anything more. She didn't want to know if Chris returned the call or what he said. After all, he'd had a life that didn't include her prior to ten days ago. She had no reason to think that there was anyone in his life to whom he owed any explanations regarding their sudden marriage.

If there was, she didn't want to hear his explanations.

When she came out of the bathroom, Chris was stretched out on the bed with his eyes closed. Since everything she owned was still packed, she had draped herself with a towel. The temptation to stretch out beside him was too much to resist, so Maribeth quietly lay down beside him.

It did feel good to rest. She would just take a few minutes to... her mind shut off and she was asleep.

Chris woke her sometime later. Freshly shaved and just out of the shower, he lay beside her, smoothing his hand over her body. She was already flushed and trembling, wanting him.

"I enjoyed waking up to find you in my bed. At first I thought for a while there I was dreaming. Then I remembered." He trailed kisses down the side of her neck until his mouth covered the tip of her breast.

In the week they'd been together, he'd discovered many ways to please her. Now he put that knowledge to work.

She could no more resist him than a flower could resist opening to the sun.

She had learned a few things, as well. By the time he moved over her, they were both trembling with need. He teased her, lowering himself slightly, then pulling away. She clasped him to her, forcing his weight down until he was inside her.

Blindly she sought his mouth, wanting to absorb him through her very pores. Her eagerness inflamed him and he took her hard and fast, racing them to their climax and toppling them into an aftermath of breathless bliss.

When he was able to speak, Chris looked at her and grinned. "So much for showering early to save time."

"We can always shower together now."

"To save time?"

She gave him an exaggerated, innocent stare. "Does it matter?"

In answer, he picked her up and carried her into the bathroom.

Seven

They were late arriving at Kenneth Cochran's palatial home, but there was still a stream of cars pulling onto the grounds when they turned onto the quiet, tree-lined street. Valet parking waited at the top of the driveway. When it was their turn, Chris helped her out of the car and handed his keys to one of the valets.

"Wow," she said under her breath, looking around at the house and extensive lawns. "How long has he lived here?"

Chris shrugged. "As far back as I can remember."

Now that was unexpected news. "You mean you were raised here?"

"Yeah."

"And your mother lived here?"

"Yes."

His replies were becoming more and more clipped. Maribeth was having trouble adjusting her views of the people involved with what she was seeing. "You're saying that your mother left this to live in Agua Verde?"

"She didn't care for the life-style."

"I get a sense that you don't, either."

"That's right. Ready to go in?"

She glanced down at the black dress she wore, which had seemed perfectly adequate when she bought it, but now she wasn't so sure. "Are you sure I look all right?"

"Maribeth, neither of us has anything to prove to these people. As a matter of fact, that provocative dress may draw more interest than you had in mind when you bought it."

"I just didn't want you to be ashamed of me."

"That could never happen. Come on."

Kenneth Cochran stood just inside the open door greeting his guests. A blond woman, who could have easily made a living as a Las Vegas show girl, stood beside him wearing a flaming red see-through dress that showcased a spectacular figure.

Kenneth spoke as soon as he spotted them. "Well, there you are. I was expecting you to be here before the others so that Maribeth and Bambi could get acquainted."

"We were unavoidably delayed," Chris stated calmly. Memories of what had delayed them caused Maribeth to blush. Bambi looked amused by her reaction. Seen up close, Bambi was stunning. She had dark blue eyes and a friendly smile.

"This is Maribeth, Bambi. I know you two are going to be good friends," Kenneth said.

Bambi held out her hand. "I can't tell you how eager I've been to meet you, Maribeth. I've been in a state of shock since Ken called me with your news. Chris had us all convinced that he never intended to marry."

Maribeth reluctantly accepted the perfectly manicured hand, immediately recognizing the sultry voice that had been on Chris's answering machine. Bambi looked at Chris. "Do I get to hug the groom?" she asked, implying a great deal more than what she said.

Chris just looked at her. She tapped him on the chest with her fist. "You never return my calls, you stinker. It's terribly rude of you."

"Blame it on my upbringing," Chris replied with a shrug.

"I'm just glad Ken was able to tell you about tonight's party. I would have hated for you to miss it." She smiled at Maribeth. "This will be a perfect occasion to announce the marriage to all our friends."

Kenneth took Chris and Maribeth by the hand, autocratically abandoning his welcoming position at the door. "Come on. There's several people I want you to meet."

In the press of people and introductions, Maribeth got separated from Chris. Eventually she wandered over to the buffet tables. She couldn't remember the last time she'd eaten. She was filling a plate with delicious-looking tidbits when Bambi appeared by her side.

"I wasn't joking, earlier, you know. You have no idea what a shock it was for me when Kenneth told me that Chris had gotten married right out of the blue like that."

"We surprised a lot of people," Maribeth answered, focusing her attention on the items displayed on the table. She hadn't eaten since a very early breakfast and now she was starved.

After a long pause, Bambi asked, "Has Chris ever spoken to you about me?"

Maribeth glanced around at her and smiled. "No."

"Oh."

Maribeth picked up her glass of wine and turned, still holding her plate. "You have a lovely place here."

"Yes," Bambi agreed absently, "It *is* nice. Is that your natural hair color?"

Maribeth hoped she hid the fact that the candid question startled her. "'Fraid so."

"It's an unusual shade."

What could she say to that?

When Maribeth made no response, Bambi asked, "How long have you known Chris?"

"Since he moved to Agua Verde when we were kids."

"Oh! That's right, he did go to school down there. He told me that once, but I'd forgotten."

"If you'll excuse me, I'm going to go find a table so I can eat." She held up the plate and glass to explain her lack of an extra hand.

Bambi followed her outside to one of the tables grouped around the Olympic-size pool. They sat down. Maribeth immediately began to eat. After a moment, Bambi said, "Chris and I used to date."

"Did you?"

"Mmm-hmm. He's terrific in bed, don't you think?"

Maribeth almost spilled her wine from the tulip-shaped glass, but managed to rescue it by clutching the stem. She could only stare at the other woman in wonder at her choice of subjects.

Obviously Maribeth's lack of conversation was not going to deter Bambi from a heart-to-heart talk about the man they had in common. "I couldn't help falling head over heels in love with him. I mean, what woman can resist him, after all? There's just something about those tall, dark, mysterious types that gets to you. I'm sure I don't have to tell you, do I? So how long were you and Chris engaged?"

"Not long."

"I just wondered, since he and I were pretty involved once upon a time. And then I met Kenneth."

"He swept you off your feet?" Maribeth offered.

"In a manner of speaking. He asked me to marry him, which was more than Chris ever did."

Maribeth was determined not to smile at the disgruntled tone.

Bambi tossed her head. "I warned Chris that I'd do it if he refused to marry me."

"Oh?"

"That was when he told me he never intended to marry."

"Ah."

"Now he shows up with you."

"Mmm."

"So you can naturally understand my surprise."

"Naturally."

"Are you pregnant?"

Maribeth was thankful she had left her wineglass alone after the first surprise. She would have spilled it for sure with that one. "We've only been married a week," she murmured.

"Don't be naive, honey. You know what I mean."

"I'm not pregnant."

Bambi nodded thoughtfully. "I thought about it, thinking that my having his baby might change his mind, but knowing Chris, he probably wouldn't have married me, anyway. Besides, he always made sure there was never a possibility of that."

A male voice immediately behind Maribeth said, "Well, I'm glad to see the two of you hitting it off so well." Kenneth Cochran pulled out one of the chairs and joined them. "I just knew you two would find you had a lot in common."

More than I could have possibly guessed, Maribeth thought to herself. She contented herself to replying to Kenneth's remark with a smile.

"Where's Chris?" Bambi asked, looking around.

"How would I know?" Kenneth answered. "I gave up trying to keep an eye on him years ago."

"I think I'll go find him," she said, jumping up from the table and dashing off.

Maribeth finished off the last stuffed mushroom on her plate and took another sip of wine.

"Have I told you that you're the most beautiful woman here tonight?" Kenneth asked.

The Cochrans were going to be the death of her yet. She almost swallowed wrong on that one. "No, sir, you haven't. I appreciate the compliment."

"Not a compliment. Just a fact. I doubt that Chris is old enough, or wise enough, to appreciate what he has in you."

"I feel very fortunate to be married to Chris."

"But he's hard to get to know. There's no denying that. That mother of his did her best to ruin him. No matter what I did, I never could get close to the kid when he was growing up."

Maribeth suddenly saw the bleakness in the man's eyes and realized that much of his brusque behavior around Chris was based on pain.

"I'm surprised you never had more children," she said after a moment.

"Are you kidding? And let them be held for ransom when the marriage ended?"

"Is that what happened with Chris?"

"Actually, no. His mother wanted no part of me or my money. She didn't want Chris anywhere around me, either, but I wouldn't let her get away with that. I fought her for custody, and lost, but at least I got him for the summers. Not that having him here did much good. He spent his time counting the days until he could return home to his friends."

"Did he ever talk to you about his life in Agua Verde?"

"Only if I cross-examined him. And then, he gave the barest details. He refused to make friends up here. He's just like his mother. There was absolutely nothing he wanted from me. As you can see, none of that has changed. Chris has never seemed close to anybody. That's why his getting married was such a shock."

Obviously there was a lot of that going around. "You didn't appear shocked. Just amused."

"Good. I would never want him to know how easily he can hurt me. Nobody wants to be thought vulnerable where another person is concerned."

"The two of you are alike in many ways."

"Don't ever let him hear you say that. He'd consider an opinion like that grounds for divorce."

"Is that what you think? That we'll end up divorced?"

"Well, I haven't set him a very good example, I'm afraid. You'd better hope he doesn't take after me in that respect."

"I would never try to hang on to him if he didn't want me, Mr. Cochran."

"Mr. Cochran? If you can't call me Dad, at least use my first name."

"What does Chris call you?"

"He makes certain he never has to address me. I can't remember the last time he called me Dad."

"I find that really sad. I lost both my parents when I was eight years old. There's nothing I can do about that. So I don't understand family members who don't attempt to get along, don't try to work out their differences. I think that family is the most precious gift we can have."

"Chris is much luckier than he knows, to have a wife who feels that way. Hopefully you can stop the Cochran cycle of discord and give Chris the love and family he needs."

"That's up to Chris, of course."

Music wafted out onto the terrace from the ballroom located in one of the wings of the house. Kenneth glanced around. "Shall we go back inside? I think you may enjoy the band I hired to play tonight. As the host, I claim the right to ask you for the first dance."

"Won't Bambi expect you to dance with her?"

He laughed, but it sounded a little forced. "Bambi? She doesn't even see me whenever Chris is around. That's not going to change."

"Is that how you met her? Through Chris?"

"More or less. He never introduced us, but I'd seen them together at various functions around town. I made a point to find out more about her. Bambi's not a bad sort at all. She came from a big family in east Texas. Never had much but her looks and she's used them to her advantage. Did she tell you she used to model?"

"No."

"Started young, got some breaks, but she hated the life. I called her one time, invited her to lunch. Told her I wanted to get to know her. It wasn't long until we were seeing each other, strictly platonic, mostly so she could complain about Chris's lack of commitment. One day, oh, I guess a year or more later, I told her that if she ever got tired of waiting for him to offer to marry her, that I would. She thought I was kidding at the time."

"But you weren't." By now, they were circling the dance floor along with a roomful of people.

"Nope. You see, I liked Bambi. She is what she is. There's no pretense about her. I like that. That's what I like about you, as well. You may have restyled your hair, found some more sophisticated clothes, but you don't pretend to be someone you're not."

"I wouldn't know how."

"Well, Bambi had the chance to go big in the modeling field, but she couldn't stand the phoniness, the backstabbing, the whole scene. So she stayed in Dallas and did quite well. Like I said, we became friends. I was tired of getting involved with women who saw me as a moneybags."

"And Bambi doesn't?"

He laughed. "Oh, I'm sure the money helped my cause a little. That and being Chris's father. She truly loves him, you know. And she wanted to be a part of his life in some capacity. Of course I could have told her that marrying me was not the way to go about it, but I had my own agenda by that time. She found out soon enough."

"How long have you been married?"

"About four months."

"Oh! Somehow, I thought it had been longer." She was quiet for a moment, wondering if she dared to say what she was thinking. Finally she said, "You really love her, don't you?"

"Oh, yes. I suppose that's why I can understand that you aren't going to have an easy time of it, being married to Chris. He's a tough man to love because he doesn't trust anyone. And how can there be love without a sense of trust?''

''Chris was helping me out of a really bad situation when he offered to marry me.''

''Nonsense. Chris married you for only one reason. He wanted to marry you. You might ask yourself why, sometime. It's my guess that you've come closer to getting through his defenses than any of us. You deserve a medal for that.''

''It's just that we've been friends for years.''

''My point, exactly. Chris doesn't have many friends. At least he allowed you into that circle.''

''We were children. He'd been living there for only a few months when my parents were killed. It was a bad time for me. He and Bobby helped me through a great deal of the pain by just being a part of my life.''

''That's good.''

''Excuse me, but may I have a dance with my wife or do you intend to monopolize her the whole evening?''

Maribeth looked around, startled by the grimness she heard in Chris's voice.

Kenneth stepped back, smiling. ''By all means. We were just getting better acquainted, son, that's all. I like your wife, Chris. Very much.''

''I've noticed,'' Chris replied, almost growling the words. He swept her into his arms and began to dance.

''I was beginning to think you'd left. I haven't seen you in some time,'' she said, her gaze on his clenched jaw.

''I hate these parties. I keep getting cornered by people.'' His gaze dropped to the scooped neck of her dress. ''I can certainly see why my father enjoyed dancing with you. From this angle, I can almost see your belly button.''

She grabbed the top of her dress. "You're kidding." She was horrified at the thought.

He circled the dance floor and she absently followed his lead.

"All that practice with my father seems to have you much more comfortable on the dance floor. Was it only a week ago when you were telling me that you didn't know how to dance?"

"I guess I wasn't paying that much attention. I was more interested in what he had to say."

"Another one of his fans, huh? Guess you and Bambi have a great deal in common."

"Actually, I had a chance to visit with her, as well."

"Oh?"

"She was reminiscing about how good you were in bed."

Chris stopped cold on the dance floor, causing another couple to bump into them. "She did what?"

"You heard me."

He took her hand and led her off the dance floor. They went through the French doors out onto the terrace. Most of the people were inside dancing. He led her to the edge of the terrace and followed a path that led to a gazebo.

He turned around and faced her. The lights from the terrace shown on his face. "I want to know exactly what Bambi said to you."

"Why?"

"Because I know her. I—"

"Yes, she did make that clear enough . . . in the Biblical sense, you mean."

"That's not what I meant. If she thought there was a chance to break us up, she'd do it."

"How could she? Whatever happened between the two of you happened before we married. Chris, don't you see? You and I have, at the most, ten days that we would need to account to each other. Anything prior to that happened before we made any commitment. From what I'm told, you aren't big on commitment."

He frowned. "What's that supposed to mean?"

"I have a much better understanding of the sacrifice you made when you offered to marry me."

"Damn it, Maribeth. I told you it wasn't a sacrifice to—"

"You gave up your privacy, Chris. I don't take that lightly. By the very nature of who you are, what you do for a living, everything about you makes it clear you don't want anyone to get close to you. Don't you realize how you've jeopardized all that by marrying me?"

He turned away from her, shoving his hands into his pockets. "I haven't jeopardized anything. I don't have anything to hide from you."

She smiled but of course he didn't see it.

"I really do like your father. I find that we have many things in common."

He spun around. "I doubt that very much. Of course he can be charming when he wants something, and it's obvious he wants your approval. Most women find him attractive. Why should you be different?"

"The most attractive thing I find about him is that he reminds me of you."

"We're nothing alike. Nothing."

"You look a great deal like him."

"I had no choice over that."

"Why do you dislike him so?"

"I have no feeling about him at all. I just prefer to live my own life. Not the one he mapped out for me."

"He chose where you lived?"

"No. My mother wanted to move back to Agua Verde. You know that."

"Then he chose the school you attended?"

"Are you kidding? He was determined I was going to go to SMU here in Dallas."

"But you chose Texas A & M so that you and Bobby and me went on to college together. I remember when we were planning that."

"So?"

"Nothing, really. I'm just thinking about how your dad has ruled your life. You said he wanted you to work with him."

He sighed. "And that's what I'm doing."

"No, you aren't. You're working *for* him, strictly as an employee, and whether he knows it or not you're there on temporary assignment for another job."

"That's true."

"What I'm sure he wanted was for you to learn the business so that he could turn it over to you someday."

"He wants control over me. He wants to dangle the business in front of me as a carrot. I refuse to bite."

"Have you ever wondered why he never had any more children?"

He turned and looked at her. "I never had to wonder. I knew. If you'd ever seen his wives, you'd know that the last thing they wanted was motherhood."

"How many times has your father been married?"

"Bambi is his third wife."

"In other words, besides your mother and Bambi, he's had one other wife. What was she like?"

"I don't remember. She was only around a few years."

"Which means your dad was single for several years before he and Bambi married."

"He may have been single, but he always had someone around to fawn over him."

Maribeth chuckled.

"What's so amusing?"

"This whole conversation, really. You didn't want to come here tonight. You want to have nothing to do with either your father or Bambi. And what I discover once I'm here are two people who love you very much."

"Is that what Bambi told you?"

"Among other things. Are you upset that she married your father?"

"I didn't care who the hell she married. I used to see her occasionally. My hours at the agency don't leave me much spare time as you're beginning to find out for yourself. Whenever I had a free evening, I'd give her a call and we'd go out. It was never anything serious, we both knew that. And yes, dammit, I made love to her a few times, which is really sickening, now that you think about it. But who would ever have guessed that she would end up becoming my stepmother?"

"Maybe it wasn't serious to you, but I have a hunch it was more than that to her."

"Nonsense. She was looking to get married. She didn't care who the fool was. My father's money was much more alluring than anything I had to offer."

"Really. She told you that?"

"She didn't have to. Once I found out they were seeing each other, I knew."

"How did you find out?"

"She told me. Of course she insisted they were just friends, which is absurd. She was just playing us one against the other."

"But you saw through her."

"That's right."

"Nobody's going to hurt you."

"You've got that right. So if you're through with all your questions, we can go home now."

"I wasn't the one who brought us out here, Chris."

"Well, I wasn't about to discuss Bambi in a roomful of people. You can rest assured that you have no reason to be jealous of her."

"I was trying to tell you that I'm not jealous of her."

He'd already started back to the house, but her words stopped him.

"Sorry, I forgot. Why should you be jealous? Your feelings for me are for a friend. There's no reason to be jealous in a friendship, is there?"

Eight

They had driven home in silence. Now Maribeth was in the bathroom removing her makeup and combing out her hair. She was getting used to her new hairstyle, and she rather liked it. It was actually just as easy to keep as the braid had been and a great deal more flattering.

Maybe she was becoming vain in her old age, but there was something energizing about knowing that she looked her best with just a few tips from experts on hair and complexion care.

If her plans worked out she would probably be too busy to worry with either in the coming months, but of course before she made definite plans, she needed to talk to Chris about them.

Chris. On the way home, he'd retreated into himself, becoming the aloof loner she'd known most of her life. She was coming to realize he used this response as a shield against hurt.

She'd never thought about how his parents' divorce had affected Chris. Would he have been a different person if his parents had stayed together? Obviously his mother had been unhappy or she would never have left his father. And his father had wanted him very, very much to have attempted to gain custody when he had no grounds.

What must all of that fighting have done to a young, sensitive child? How could he grow up with the two people he most closely identified with fighting each other without being scarred by it?

That was what she realized tonight. She'd learned a great deal about her new husband, seeing him in his father's home in Dallas, hearing about how his father felt about him, and meeting Bambi.

It was obvious that Kenneth and Bambi Cochran had an unusual relationship with each other, but no matter what the world thought, they were good for each other, and good to each other.

Granted, Maribeth had never met a woman like Bambi. If she had been Kenneth, she wouldn't have been quite so tolerant of the woman's obvious feelings for his son.

What Maribeth was beginning to understand was that there were all kinds of people in the world, each one with a specific upbringing that molded and shaped his or her personality. Wouldn't she be considerably different from who she was today if her parents had lived? She'd probably have another sister or two, possibly brothers as well. She was certain she wouldn't have been pampered as much as Megan and Mollie had pampered her.

Even Travis and Deke had made a definite impression on her perspective, especially regarding men. Whether she'd been aware of it or not, these past few years she had begun to compare Bobby with her brothers-in-law and found that his refusal to commit to their marriage was a bad sign.

When Megan agreed to marry Travis, he'd wanted to plan an immediate wedding, even though he was still following the rodeo circuit. It's true that he'd quit traveling the following year, but he'd made it clear that he wanted to stay home.

Bobby was such a child. Just as she had been. Just as she still was, in so many ways. Chris, on the other hand, had never had the chance to be a child. He'd acted like an adult as far back as she could remember.

Somehow, someway, she wanted to give him back his childhood. Was it even possible?

She opened the door into the bedroom and discovered that Chris wasn't in there. Maybe he'd gotten tired of waiting and used the bathroom down the hall. Peering into the hallway, she saw that a downstairs light was on.

She went downstairs and found him in the kitchen, eating a bowl of macaroni and cheese.

"Hi," she said, sitting across from him.

He glanced up, his eyes shadowed. "Hi, yourself."

"Didn't you eat at your father's?"

"I wasn't hungry then."

"Ah."

"I like your hair that way."

"I'm glad. So do I. The man who cut it said that it will have a tendency to wave more now that it's been layered. The weight of the length pulled out any natural curl I might have." She knew she was chattering, but she wanted to chase his dark mood away.

"I want you to be happy, Maribeth."

So much for chasing a mood away. "I am happy. Can't you see that? I couldn't be happier."

"I tricked you into marrying me."

She eyed him warily. "How did you do that? Were you lying when you said that Bobby called to say he'd gotten married?"

"No."

"Then what was the trick?"

"Offering to marry you when you were too emotional to make a rational decision."

"I was pretty emotional, all right."

"And I took advantage of that."

"I knew what I was doing."

"Not really."

"Let's put it another way, then. I would say that I'm rational at the moment, and I in no way regret having married you."

"You don't?"

"Not at all."

A glimmer of a smile appeared. "I'm glad to hear it."

"You mean you were actually worried about it?"

"Yeah. I feel like I stole you away from the life you had and loved and brought you up here to a cast of characters that are too bizarre to be believed."

Encouraged by his smile, she asked, "What does your dad think you've been doing since you graduated from college?"

"As little as possible. I've had odd jobs on various covert assignments and he found out about them. Because he didn't know they were covers, he was irritated that I was wasting my education and talents."

"You could have told him the truth."

"Maybe, although too much talk can hurt you in this business."

"But he's your father, for Pete's sake."

"Yeah, so you've pointed out a time or two."

"Do you really suspect him of being a part of this latest assignment?"

"I've already told you, I can't discuss the assignment with you. Not now. Not ever."

"Fair enough. Just tell me this. How are you going to feel if you end up arresting your father?"

"If he's doing something illegal, he deserves whatever happens to him."

"So you wouldn't care."

"I didn't say that."

"I can't tell you how relieved I am to hear you say that," she replied. Looking around the kitchen, she asked, "Where did you get the macaroni and cheese?"

"Out of a package I cooked up. There's more on the stove if you want some."

She hopped up and found a bowl and put a small amount inside. "I need to make a grocery list and start planning some meals around here."

"Only if you want."

"I want. Don't you understand, Chris? I want to be a wife to you."

"You already are. You've got my ring on your finger to prove it."

She stuck her tongue out at him and he grinned. Then they both laughed.

Later, when they went upstairs, Chris made slow, exquisitely sensual love to her in ways she could never have imagined until he had her pleading for mercy from the onslaught. She forgot their conversations that evening in the heat of the moment, only to recall them in the days ahead when she worked at setting up a routine around his schedule.

She'd forgotten to tell him her idea about what she could do with her time now that she was living in Dallas.

It was Friday before she'd decided how to bring up the subject. It was easy enough to plan his favorite dinner. She'd bought the T-bone steaks earlier that day. She intended to have him grill them over charcoals outside while she fried potatoes and made a big salad.

When the doorbell rang, she assumed it was a salesman of some sort and hurried to answer it. It was almost four o'clock. She was expecting Chris home before long.

She opened the door and then stood there in shock, thankful she had the solid door to hang on to. The man standing there looked just as shocked.

"Maribeth?"

"Bobby?"

"What are you doing here?" they both said at the same time.

Bobby looked ashen and she wondered if he was going to faint. Maribeth could certainly relate to the feeling.

"If you've come to see Chris, he isn't here, but I expect him soon. Would you like to come inside and wait for him?"

She looked past him and saw his truck sitting in the driveway. There was no one in it. She looked back at him and noticed that his face now looked flushed with embarrassment.

"You're the last person I ever expected to open that door," he drawled, his gaze not quite meeting hers.

"Why don't you come inside, Bobby? It's too hot to stand here with the door open."

"Oh, yeah. Sure." He walked inside, taking off his hat and turning it in his hands by the brim.

"Come on back to the kitchen. I'll fix you some tea if you'd like."

Bobby cleared his throat. "Yeah. Thanks. I could use something to drink. I've been driving for several hours."

She'd been cleaning house today and still wore her oldest clothes and a scarf around her hair. She could at least take the scarf off, she decided, tugging at it on the way to the kitchen.

"You cut your hair," he said, following her into the room.

"Yes."

He seemed to be studying everything about her without once meeting her gaze. Seeing how uncomfortable he was made her feel a little better. Actually a lot better. He looked tired.

She hadn't seen him in months. She wondered if she'd ever actually looked at him when he came home, or whether she saw the man she wanted to see. Looking at the man who had sat down on one of the bar stools, she was aware of a great many changes from the boy she'd grown up with.

Without the gauzy transparency of hero worship that she'd always wrapped around him, he was quite ordinary. He seemed shorter, but that was probably because she was used to being with Chris. His hair had darkened from blond to a light brown. His eyes were as blue as ever, startling in his deeply tanned face. She'd always loved his eyes.

She turned away and began to chop vegetables to go into the salad she'd planned.

"What are you doing here, Maribeth? You're the last person I ever expected to find here."

"Having a little trouble facing me, are you?"

"What's that supposed to mean?"

"Oh, there's the little matter of a wedding date that was set a couple of weeks ago."

"Hell. Didn't Chris tell you I wouldn't be there? Damn it, I specifically called him so that he'd let you know—"

"Why didn't *you* let me know, Bobby? You were the man I was going to marry. Why didn't you tell me you'd changed your mind?"

"Because I didn't change my mind! Hell, I've been planning to marry you ever since we were in junior high. There was never anybody else and you know it."

"I see." She continued to chop vegetables without looking up from the task. "I guess Chris must have gotten your message confused about being in Las Vegas and marrying somebody else."

Bobby stood and walked over to the sliding doors that led to the patio area. "No. He wasn't confused. I was just too ashamed to tell you."

"I can understand why. It was a shameful thing to pull, Bobby."

He turned and looked at her, his eyes haunted. "You think I don't know that? You think I haven't faced it every single day since then? You think I haven't remembered all the plans we made together, all the things we've done together, all the dreams we had? I went a little haywire, that's all. It was just a normal thing at first, getting jittery about finally getting hitched. And I've really been on a roll lately, winning my rounds, racking up the points. I guess I was scared that everything was going to change."

What could she say to that?

Bobby cleared his throat. In a gruff voice, he said, "If it makes you feel any better, I want you to know I'm sorry for hurting you. You never deserved that."

"I agree. I never did."

"Maribeth, you're still just as much a part of me as one of my arms or legs. I haven't felt the same since—"

"Well, hello, Bobby," Chris said from the doorway of the garage, "what a surprise to see you here."

Bobby spun around with a tremendous look of relief on his face. "Chris! There you are! I was passing through Dallas and was hoping I could crash here for the night. I didn't know you already had company. I guess you can imagine how surprised I was to find Maribeth here."

Maribeth could feel Chris's gaze on her, but she refused to look up. Instead she slipped the salad she'd just completed into the refrigerator and began to peel the potatoes for the French fries.

"Where's your wife, Bobby?" Chris asked, going to the refrigerator and reaching inside for two bottles of beer. He handed one to Bobby who looked grateful enough to cry.

"I, uh, well. That whole thing was just sort of a lark." He darted a glance at Maribeth. "I mean, hell, Chris, you know how it is. We'd all been drinking and—"

"That happens fairly often with you these days, doesn't it, Bobby? That's a way to get yourself killed on one of those bulls."

Bobby grinned, looking cocky. "I never drink before I'm going to ride. You know me better than that, Chris."

"I thought I did."

Bobby flushed. "Yeah. I was just telling Maribeth here how sorry I am for hurting her."

"I'm sure she appreciates hearing about your feelings on the matter."

"The thing is, Leona and I—well, neither one of us was really thinking clearly. We knew after a couple of days that us being a couple would never work out. She's already talking about getting an annulment. She took off for Montana a week ago."

Maribeth refused to look at Chris but she could feel his eyes on her.

"Sorry to hear that," he said. "Why don't you come outside with me? I need to start some coals for the grill." He stepped outside and held the door open for Bobby. "I've got some good-looking T-bones in there I plan to charcoal. Think you could wrap yourself around one of them?"

Bobby followed him out so quickly it was almost more than Maribeth could do not to laugh out loud. It was obvious the man couldn't get far enough away from her.

"Oh, no, that's all right," she heard Bobby say. "You've already made plans and all. I don't want to butt into anything."

"You aren't butting in, Bobby. It's good to see you again. You know you're always welcome to stay here whenever you're in town. It's just been a while, hasn't it?"

Maribeth recognized the subtle tone of amusement in Chris's voice. He was enjoying seeing how uncomfortable Bobby was as much as she had been. Not that Bobby didn't deserve a little squirming for the way he'd handled the matter.

And he wasn't even going to stay married!

What a narrow escape she'd had. It was almost scary to think about the fact that she could easily be married to Bobby right now and it could be Chris who had come to visit.

The thought sobered her. The suggestion that she would not be married to Chris Cochran was frightening. Tomorrow was their second-week anniversary. In fact, Bobby Metcalf was their very first guest.

How was that for being bizarre?

She'd expected to hate Bobby forever. She'd expected never to want to see him again, but that hadn't been the case at all. The truth was, seeing him again didn't matter to her one way or the other. Bobby was just somebody she'd known for ages. She had no feelings at seeing him...not anger, not pain, not even pleasure. She might have spent her life with a giant-size crush on him, but she'd never really seen him as a person, a friend.

Not like Chris, who had always been there for her.

Funny how things turn out.

She glanced at the time. She still had a few minutes before she needed to start the fries. Once the grease was hot, they would cook in minutes. Maribeth slipped upstairs to shower and change clothes for dinner. After all, they were entertaining for the first time and she wanted to look her best.

Chris noticed that Maribeth had left the kitchen when he came inside to get the steaks. He felt bad that he hadn't greeted her when he got home. Seeing Bobby Metcalf standing there in his kitchen talking to his wife had unnerved him considerably.

Until he'd looked at Maribeth. She was handling Bobby's visit just fine, considering that his appearance must have been just as much a shock to her as it was to him.

She'd been wearing her old clothes, and from the looks of the house, she'd spent the day cleaning. He wasn't too surprised that she'd decided to get spruced up for their company.

He had a hunch that Bobby was going to have several shocks coming to him as the evening progressed. Chris couldn't think of anyone more deserving.

* * *

He waited until he saw that Maribeth was back in the kitchen before putting the steaks on the grill. A few minutes later she walked out holding a tray.

"I thought we could eat out here tonight, if you'd like." She brought dishes and silverware and a salad. He hurried over to help her with the tray.

She'd changed into one of her new dresses, a sundress with tiny straps across the shoulders and a full skirt that was short enough to show off those sexy legs of hers. She'd also done something to her hair, pulling it away from her face so that it fell in a cascade of waves and curls down her neck and shoulders.

She looked as sexy as hell and his body immediately responded. A quick glance at Bobby made it clear that Maribeth's new look had thrown him yet again.

"My God, Maribeth. Woman, you're dynamite in that outfit." Bobby swore softly. "Don't you agree, Chris?"

Chris took the tray from Maribeth and winked at her before turning back to Bobby. "Oh, Maribeth knows what I think about her."

Bobby was already up and trying to help her set the table. "Well, of course. We've all been friends for years but damn, honey, I've never seen you looking so...so..."

"You've probably never seen me in a dress."

Bobby laughed. "That could be it. I had no idea your legs were, I mean—"

"I think we know what you mean," Chris replied. "Ready for another beer?"

Obviously distracted, Bobby said, "Sure," while he tried to engage Maribeth in conversation. Chris went back into the house, deliberately leaving them alone.

So Bobby wasn't going to stay married and it was more than a little obvious that he was knocked off his feet by

Maribeth's new image. The idiot hadn't noticed that he and Maribeth were wearing matching wedding bands. Chris wondered if he was going to have to say something to him, or whether Maribeth would.

Dinner was pleasant enough. Bobby was much more relaxed after the beers he'd had, and he was entertaining them with stories he'd seen and heard on the road. Without being totally conscious of it, the three of them had fallen into their old camaraderie. And why not? They'd been friends for most of their lives.

Chris was comfortable with the situation because he knew that Bobby had used up all of his chances with Maribeth. He could also see that she had come to grips with the kind of relationship she and Bobby had shared, and it was nothing like theirs.

He and Maribeth could talk. They understood each other. Maribeth understood him better than anyone in his life. He'd realized that at his father's party. He hadn't forgotten the questions she'd asked him and the way they pointed out his biased thinking toward his father and how he viewed what had happened to him in his youth.

Supposing, just supposing, that his father really loved him. If that were the case, then Chris had done and said some very hurtful things to the man over the years.

It was only because of his expanding relationship with Maribeth that he had the courage to reevaluate his relationship with his father and accept his own responsibility for the fact that it hadn't been a good one.

"Would you like a piece of pie?"

Maribeth interrupted his reverie. Chris raised his brows. "Pie? On top of all of this? No, thanks." He eyed her with a grin. "Thought you couldn't cook."

"I'm not really good at it, but Mollie taught me how to bake a few things."

Bobby was leaning back in his chair, looking relaxed. He gave Maribeth his killer smile and said, "You never did tell me what you're doing visiting up here with Chris, honey. I'm surprised Megan would stand for it."

Maribeth began to clear the table, carefully stacking the dishes on the tray she'd brought out earlier. "I'm over twenty-one, Bobby. Megan doesn't have any say-so over me."

"Maybe not legally, but I bet she had a few things to say about your coming up here."

Maribeth looked at Chris and grinned. "Yeah, she did."

"But it didn't stop you."

"No."

"I should have had you go on the road with me. You'd love it, honey. Maybe one of these days you'd like to—"

"I don't think so," Chris said quietly.

Bobby glanced at Chris in surprise. "Come on, Chris. You know me better than to think I'd take advantage of her. Hell, in all these years I've never—"

"Yes, I know you've never, which is the only thing that saved our friendship."

Bobby straightened in his chair. "Hey, Chris. I know what I did was wrong, but I've apologized. Maribeth knows how I feel."

"Did you ever bother to ask her how she dealt with the fact that you disappeared on her three days before her wedding? Did you ever wonder how she was able to face everyone in Agua Verde and tell them what you had done?"

Bobby squirmed. "Well, I'm sure it wasn't easy. I figure I'm going to have to steer clear of the place for a while until something else happens for everybody to gossip about." He turned to Maribeth. "I guess I just figured you'd handle things like you always have."

"Actually, Chris was a big help."

"That's good. I guess that's what friends are for, to help out." He made a great show of stretching and yawning. "Look, I've really enjoyed visiting with y'all, but I've been on the road for hours and I'm really beat. I don't mind sacking out on the sofa. I've slept on harder surfaces before."

Chris said, "There's no reason to do that, Bobby. You know where the guest bedroom is. You're welcome to use it."

"Oh. Well, I just figured that...well...with Maribeth here and all, that she was sleeping in there."

Maribeth gave Bobby that friendly full-of-sunshine smile that always made Chris's heart soar with love for her and said, "Oh, no, Bobby. I'm sleeping with Chris."

Nine

Maribeth was already in bed when Chris finally came into the bedroom. He closed the door behind him, then leaned against it, looking at her.

"Well?" she asked.

"The guy's heartbroken."

She laughed. "Of course he is."

Chris pushed away from the door. "Actually there's every likelihood he is." He walked over to the bed and sat down, pulling his shoes and socks off. "The one constant in his life has always been you, Maribeth. Over the years you've accepted him without reservation, forgiven him time after time when he was thoughtless or self-absorbed. He took you for granted. He's probably never thought about a life without you in it somewhere. If the truth were known, I have a strong hunch that Bobby stopped by here tonight to get the lay of the land where you were concerned. Finding you here was a shock, it was true, but by the time dinner was over, he was already convinced that he'd gotten back into your good graces."

"Surely even Bobby isn't that insensitive."

He laughed at the disbelief in her voice. He stood long enough to take off the rest of his clothes, then slid into bed next to her. "I don't think it ever occurred to him that you could look at another man."

"Much less sleep with one." She curled up on his shoulder.

"Exactly." He trailed his fingers down her spine and was rewarded with her sigh of contentment.

"So the shock was pretty intense, huh?"

"Yeah."

She brushed her lips across his. "Tough."

"My sentiments, exactly."

She straightened so that she could see his face. "We're no longer kids playing games, Chris. I would have thought he'd know that."

"Bobby's beginning to get the picture now, anyway." He pulled her across him so that she straddled his body. From this position he had a full range of motion to sculpt and shape her breasts. He took full advantage of it. "He had his chance and he blew it."

She ran her hands over his chest. "Oh, Chris," she whispered. "It scares me to think how close I came to making a horrible mistake."

"Then you don't consider our marriage a mistake?"

"Not at all."

"Even if I send you home tomorrow?"

Her hands stopped. "What do you mean, home? I am home."

"I want you to go to Agua Verde for a few days. This assignment I'm on is about ready to blow, which means I've got to make myself scarce for the next week or so. I want you to be unavailable as well."

"Couldn't I just go with you?"

"You're too distracting."

"I certainly hope so."

"You can take my car."

"Your beautiful baby? Are you sure you can live without it?"

"No. But I'm going to do my best."

"You trust me to drive it?"

"I trust you totally."

"When do I have to go?"

"In the morning. You may not have noticed, but I actually came home early tonight so we'd have this evening together, since this would be our last one for a while."

"It's going to be dangerous, isn't it, Chris?"

"C'mon, Maribeth. It's a job and I'm trained to do it. It's just that I don't want to worry about you."

"Why would you do that?"

"I don't know. Guess it's just a habit of mine I can't seem to break. So. Will you go visit your family?" He lifted her, positioning her over him, then smoothly entered her.

She wriggled with pleasure and sighed, gently rocking on him. "Married two weeks and you're already trying to get rid of me."

He was having a little trouble breathing and more trouble concentrating. "But it was a great two weeks," he managed to say.

"Mmm," she agreed, moving more rapidly.

"And when, umm, this is...o-over...we'll have plenty...m-m-m-more."

"I'll remind you of that—" she whispered urgently "—as well as of this."

It was a long time later and they were almost asleep before Maribeth remembered to ask, "How long will I have to be gone?"

"Hopefully no more than a few days."

She curled into him a little closer. "At least I'll have some really good memories to take with me."

He held her for the longest time, staring into the dark. Would she want to have anything to do with him, once she found out what he'd been doing?

By the time Maribeth left the Dallas city limits she was in love with Chris's car. She couldn't believe how fun it was to drive. How responsive it was. It carried the faint scent of Chris's after-shave, which she savored.

She missed him already. He'd been gone when she woke up that morning, but he'd left her a note telling her that he would be in touch and for her not to worry. She didn't even know how he'd managed to leave, since she had the car. She had forgotten to ask so many things the night before. He must have had someone pick him up.

Telling her not to worry was like telling her not to think about the black horse. If he hadn't mentioned it, she might not have thought about it. Now she could think of nothing else.

She just kept feeling a sense of uneasiness, the farther south she drove. What was it? It didn't have anything to do with Bobby, she knew that. He, too, was gone. She'd heard his truck drive away before daylight.

What a sense of freedom there had been for her when she realized that although she may have loved Bobby, she really didn't like him. He'd fallen in with a rambunctious crowd that encouraged his wildness. What had been attractive to her in the young boy and rowdy teenager was much less attractive to her in the grown man.

She was at peace now. She had a husband who was attentive, attractive and adorable. What more could she possibly want?

Love?

Where had that come from? Of course she loved Chris. Why, she had loved him for years. Maybe she hadn't understood her feelings for him at the time. How could she, through that haze of hero worship around Bobby?

What she didn't understand, and could not help wondering about, was how Chris felt about her. If his actions were any indication, he was attracted to her, felt comfortable with her, enjoyed her company.

So why is he sending you away?

That has something to do with his job, and the fact that their marriage had come at an awkward time in his work. She tried to put the idea that he was finding his marriage inconvenient out of her mind.

She wanted to see her family again anyway. Chris had just offered her the opportunity to do so. Stop imagining problems where they don't exist, she muttered to herself, glad to see from a sign she'd just passed that she didn't have too much farther to go.

As soon as she parked the car in front of the ranch house, there was a clamor of children's voices. "It's Maribeth! Mama, look who's here. It's Maribeth!"

In addition to Megan's three, she also spotted Mollie's three racing around the yard. Good. Mollie must be over visiting. She'd timed her arrival perfectly.

"Hi, guys," she said, after carefully closing the gate behind her. "Looks like you've been having fun."

Each one of them had something to share with her, so it took her a while to reach the porch, climb the stairs and get inside the kitchen door.

"Y'all go on and play now," Megan said, when they tried to follow her into the house, "and let Maribeth rest for a minute. You can see her later." She turned to Maribeth and grinned. "Well, my goodness, honey. I don't have to ask how you like married life. It's obvious that it's agreeing with you. You look scrumptious."

She hugged her, then motioned to one of the kitchen chairs. "Sit down and let me get you something to drink. Tea, soda, lemonade, you name it."

"Iced tea sounds wonderful."

Then they both asked at the same time,

"Where's Chris?"

"Where's Mollie?"

Both tried to answer at the same time, then burst out laughing. Megan said, "You first. What did you do with your new husband?"

"He was really busy with work and suggested I might want to take some time to come visit. It sounded like a good idea to me. I've got so much to tell you and Mollie, about Chris's dad, our honeymoon in Atlanta and Miami, the new house and seeing Bobby." She paused for a breath. "But I don't want to have to tell it all twice." She looked around again. "Is Mollie upstairs?"

Megan set two glasses and a plate of cookies on the table. "She's not here. I offered to keep the children today, more for Deke's peace of mind than anything."

Maribeth straightened. "What's wrong? What's happened?"

Megan grinned. "Nothing much. Mollie fainted yesterday and scared Deke half to death. 'Course he rushes her to the doctor's office right away and they found out she's a few weeks pregnant."

"Mollie's pregnant again? I thought Deke absolutely swore she wasn't going through all that again."

"What he means is *he* can't go through all of it again, but it looks like he's going to have to, 'cause the doctor confirmed it. I guess there's no guarantee with any method short of doing without and Mollie made it clear she wasn't going to stand for that. Of course, she's thrilled to death. She'd have a dozen if she could."

"Amy's four now. So she shouldn't have too much trouble with a new one to care for."

"That's what I told Deke. The man's not rational where Mollie's concerned, especially not after losing his first wife shortly after she gave birth to Jolene."

"I thought that given enough time, he'd get over his fear."

"Not Deke. He demanded that Mollie stay in bed for a couple of days to rest. The doctor admitted she was probably pushing herself a little and bed rest wouldn't hurt."

"Guess your hands are full, with all of them."

"Travis helps to keep an eye on them. Plus I still have help several times a week. I don't mind."

"I wonder if I could stay with Mollie for a few days and look after things for her?"

"A few days! I thought you just came for an overnight."

"Chris talked as though he'd be tied up all week."

"Oh." Megan studied her younger sister for a long while. "Are you sure things are okay? You said you'd seen Bobby."

"Oh, yes. As a matter of fact, he dropped by to see Chris yesterday. He had no idea I was there. And when he saw me he assumed I was up there visiting a friend. It never occurred to him that Chris and I were married."

"I can understand that. You caught everyone by surprise with that one."

"I have to admit that it was rather pleasing to be able to face Bobby in such a way. Even if he didn't want me, he found out that someone else did."

"I can understand how you feel, but getting married out of spite isn't the greatest basis on which to build a relationship."

"I know, Megan. But Chris and I have more than that together."

"I'm glad to hear it." She finished her tea and stood. "I've got to check on the children. You might give Mollie a call and let her know you're here."

"Better than that. I think I'll drive over and surprise her."

"Will you be back for supper?"

"Maybe not. I could stay over there and make something. Is Deke picking up his gang?"

"Yes. I tried to get him to let them stay overnight but he said he could handle them once he was through today. He planned his time so that he could stay close to home for the rest of the week."

"Then he can use some help feeding them." She gave her sister a quick hug. "I'll see you later."

She found Mollie in the kitchen when she arrived at her home. "Deke's going to tie you to that bed if he catches you up," she said by way of greeting through the screen door.

Mollie spun around and gave a little squeak. "Oh, Maribeth, I didn't hear you drive up." She chuckled. "And you're right. Deke would be hollering if he saw me up. But darn it, I'm always wanting something to snack on. So I snuck out of bed." She gave Maribeth a big hug. "You're looking great, baby sister. I take it Megan filled you in on my news."

"Oh, yes. I'm so thrilled for you."

"I am, too. It was an accident. I swear it was, but I'm not sorry to be pregnant. I've just got to convince Deke that I'll be all right. However, after this one, I have a hunch he'll make sure I can't get pregnant again."

"Maybe you'll have another boy, so you'll have two pair."

"I don't care what it is, as long as it's healthy. I just look forward to having a baby in the house again." She grabbed a bowl of fruit and said, "Come on back and talk to me. Deke will be pleased you're here to keep me company and I want to hear about everything that's happened to you since you left."

Maribeth trailed behind her sister down the hallway and into the bedroom. Mollie looked pale. Knowing her, Maribeth could imagine that she was trying to do the work of three people around there.

"I'll talk for a little while, but then I want to start dinner so that it will be ready when Deke gets back with the children."

"Oh, you don't have to do that."

"I know, but I want to. I'm only beginning to realize how spoiled I was all these years, letting you and Megan do most of the work."

Mollie stretched out on the bed and folded her hands across her stomach, a tiny smile playing around her mouth. She listened while Maribeth described the plane, and Kenneth, the flights, the hotels, and Chris's home. Then she told her about Bobby's visit.

"What I don't understand is why Chris sent you down here. A lot of men work long hours, but that doesn't mean their wives have to leave home."

"I guess it's because I'm so new there and don't know anyone. Our marriage was so unexpected that he wasn't ready to have me there on a full-time basis. But it's only for a few days. We're both adjusting to being married to each other."

"Didn't you say he flew one of the company planes for his father?"

"Yes, but he also works for the government as one of the agents dealing with the drug problems we're having." Maribeth looked away for a moment. "I'm not supposed to tell anyone about that part, so please don't say anything to anybody. I have a hunch that what he does is really dangerous."

"Maribeth, what have you gotten yourself into?"

"I'm not sure, Mollie, and that's the truth."

"Your impulsiveness has always worried me, but I was hoping you were growing out of it."

"I'm really lucky that it was Chris who came to my rescue."

"But when are you going to get to the point in your life that you don't need to be rescued, that you don't need to be sent somewhere to be looked after?"

"Actually I'm hoping you'll let me look after you, at least for a few days."

"Of course you're welcome here. The children adore you. We all do. I guess I still see you as a child."

"Even though I'm only two years younger than you."

"Yes. Even then."

"Once Chris has more time to spend with me, I intend to tell him about my idea for something for me to do up there. His place is large enough to have a small horse barn and a couple of paddocks. I'm thinking about checking to see if I can work with a couple of horses at a time, maybe boarding or possibly training. That's what I love to do and I noticed that out where Chris lives there are several places with horses."

"You haven't mentioned it to Chris yet?"

"No. We really haven't had much time with each other."

"You're happy with him?"

"Oh, yes."

"Then that's what counts, Maribeth. I want to see you happy."

Hours later Maribeth sat at the dining room with the family laughing at the antics of the children as they told their mom and dad about their day. She enjoyed the children so much. That was something she and Chris hadn't talked about, but she hoped he wanted a family.

There were many things they hadn't talked about. Since their marriage they had been on a glamorous honeymoon and played house a few days. Now she was back in Agua Verde and having trouble not thinking her life with Chris had been a very pleasant dream.

They were eating dessert when she thought she heard the name "Cochran" mentioned on the television in the other room. The children had forgotten to turn it off when they were called to supper.

She hastily excused herself and went into the other room. The news had on-the-scene reporters discussing something that was going on in Dallas. Just as she reached the television, a shot of Kenneth Cochran was flashed on the screen. She listened in shock as the news anchor announced, "Kenneth Cochran, well-known businessman was one of several men arrested today on charges of being part of a widespread money-laundering system that spread from Florida to Texas. Mr. Cochran's attorney has refused all interviews on behalf of his client, other than to say that the charges are unfounded and will be easily disproved. Because of the amount of money involved in this case, and because federal investigators fear that he might try to leave the country if released on bail, Kenneth Cochran is being held without bail. We'll have the latest sports update after this word."

Maribeth stared blankly at the screen while an animated commercial flashed in front of her. Mollie spoke from behind her. "That was Chris's father, wasn't it?"

"Yes," she whispered.

"Do you think Chris knows about it?"

She turned and faced Mollie, her heart pounding. "Oh, Mollie, I think he's one of the investigators that helped to arrest him!"

Mollie looked horrified. "He had his own father arrested?"

"He really dislikes his father. I tried to get him to talk to me about his feelings, but you know Chris. He never lets anyone close to him."

"But do you think he's guilty?"

"How would I know? I just met the man. I know he has money. Lots of money. I never questioned where it came from. Oh, Mollie, I've got to call Chris. I need to talk to him."

"Use the phone in Deke's office. You'll have more privacy there."

Maribeth called their house but no one answered. When the machine came on, she said, "Chris, this is Maribeth. I'm at Mollie's. I'll be staying here." She gave the number. "Please call me as soon as you come home."

She hung up slowly, wondering if she could have said something more. Wondering what she could have said. What was Chris feeling now that all of this had happened?

She waited until almost midnight before getting ready for bed. He'd never returned her call. Before going to sleep, she decided to call him once again. This time the phone rang and rang but the machine didn't pick up. Had he been home and disconnected it? There was no way to know. She could only wait until he called her.

The next several days were like living in a nightmare to Maribeth. As more and more reporters dug into the story, it filled more and more news spots and newspapers. Three weekly magazines had lengthy articles on the money-laundering scheme.

It hadn't taken them long to discover a federal investigator by the name of Cochran had worked on the case and that he was the son of the man arrested. The media had a field day with that one.

They kept referring to Chris as the mysterious federal agent because no one had been able to locate him for an interview. They found a photograph of him that was shown with every news update. They'd even discovered that he had recently married, but so far hadn't been able to locate Maribeth. A few reporters had reached the two ranches but Travis and Deke quickly made it clear they wouldn't tolerate having their lives disrupted over the media's need to make news out of any and everything.

By far the worst thing was that Chris had never gotten back in touch with Maribeth. Not once since she'd left Dallas.

By Friday night, she was beginning to wonder if he had ever intended to stay in touch with her. She'd had six days to think about the two weeks she'd spent with Chris, to remember everything he had said and done, to remember all that he hadn't said and done. Never once had he talked about his feelings for her, other than to point out their friendship. He'd never talked about their future together.

He'd made love to her as though he cared for her, but then, she had no way of knowing or comparing what had happened between them with the way a man treated the woman he loved. But if Chris loved her, wouldn't he have said so? Had she been so naive as to take his feelings for her for granted without questioning him?

By Saturday she was numb. They'd been married for three weeks. She hadn't seen or spoken to him in a week, one-third the length of their marriage.

The phone rang sometime after eleven that night. Everyone in the family was in bed but Maribeth wasn't asleep. She hadn't been able to sleep much all week.

She heard a tap on the door. "Maribeth?" It was Deke. "Chris is on the phone."

She leaped out of the bed as though it were on fire, grabbed her robe and ran down the hall to Deke's office.

"Hello, Chris? Where are you?" she asked, out of breath.

His deep voice sounded tired. "That doesn't matter. I just wanted to see how you were."

"Upset that I haven't heard from you. What's going on? How is your dad? How are you? Why haven't you called?"

She heard him clear his throat. "I've been doing some serious thinking about us, and I really think it would be a good idea for you to talk to a lawyer."

"A lawyer! Why?"

"He can explain the law to you. He'll be able to tell you whether you can file for an annulment or whether you'll have to file for a divorce."

Maribeth's knees buckled and she sank to the floor beside the desk. "You're saying you want a divorce?"

There was a long pause. "I, uh, yeah, that's really what I'm saying. I'm sorry the way things worked out for us. I don't think either one of us gave much thought to our future together. It would never have worked out. We should have seen that."

She clutched the phone so tightly her fingers ached. "I don't agree with you, Chris." She could feel her heart pounding like a drum and she wondered if he could hear it as well. "I think we were getting along fine. We weren't having any problems that I could see."

He didn't answer right away and she couldn't think of anything more to say. Finally he said, "The thing is, Maribeth, I'm not cut out for marriage. I've always known that. I thought I could help you out as a friend, but I...I can't follow through in the long haul. Besides, once Bobby's free maybe the two of you can—"

"Have you been drinking, Chris Cochran?" she demanded. "What's the matter with you? You were there. You saw what Bobby's like these days. He's still a teenager, and an immature one at that! Couldn't you see how relieved I was that I didn't marry him, how grateful I am that I married you?"

"Well, I'll accept your gratitude. I'm glad I could help out, but you need to be with someone like yourself. Someday you're going to meet the man who can give you everything you want and deserve."

"*You* gave me everything I could ever want, Chris, and much more than I ever deserved."

"Including a name that's been splashed across the United States."

"Is that what this is all about? Do you honestly think I care what's being said about you, or about Kenneth?"

"If you don't, you should be. This whole thing has blown up in ways no one could have predicted. It may cost me my job. I may end up being indicted myself. There's been suggestions that I was part of the deal, playing both sides."

"But that's not true."

"How do you know, Maribeth? You don't know me or what I'm capable of. I could have been lying to you from the very beginning. Look, let's try to salvage the friendship, okay? I don't want to lose that. Go talk to a lawyer. Tell him I'll pay his fee, whatever it is. Let's put this behind us and get on with our lives."

"You can't mean it, Chris. I thought that you—"

"That I what?"

"I thought that you loved me."

"You were my childhood friend. Of course I loved you."

She closed her eyes in an effort to stop the tears that were rolling down her cheeks.

"I never tried to be something I wasn't with you, Maribeth. I tried my damnedest to be straight with you."

"I know."

"Look, I've got to let you go. Keep the car if you want. I'm not going to need it. I'll send you money each month to—"

"For what?"

"You're my wife. I'll pay your bills until—"

"No, you won't. If you don't want to stay married to me, fine. I'm not going to hang on to you if you want to be free. But I'm not going to take money from you. If this is what you want, then let's make it a clean break. I'm sorry you feel the way you do. But I'm not going to fight you."

"Take care of yourself, okay? Let me hear from you. If you ever need anything, let me know."

"Goodbye, Chris."

She sat in the dark on the floor, cradling the phone in her arms. How strange. Within a few weeks both of the men in her life—the only men in her life other than her brothers-in-law—had made it clear they didn't want her as part of their lives.

What was the flaw in her that they could see so clearly that she'd never known was there? What was so wrong with her? How could she have reached this age and not understood that she had nothing that a man wanted?

Of course she wasn't going to keep his car. She wanted nothing that reminded her of him. Tomorrow she would drive it back to Dallas and leave it at his home. She still had a key to the house. She would drive back, pack the rest of her things, get a cab to the airport and fly back to Austin. She'd get Travis or Megan to meet her plane.

All right. She probably deserved this. She'd had too much pride to admit that Bobby had spurned her, so she had jumped into marriage with Chris. At least she still had enough pride not to beg him to reconsider.

If he didn't want her, she'd learn to accept it. Somehow. But not tonight. Tonight she could only feel the pain of losing the man she'd only recently discovered she loved with all her heart.

Ten

The weather appeared to be sympathizing with her mood. It had been raining on her steadily since she'd left Austin on Interstate 35 and headed north. By the time she reached Dallas she felt that the sky had been crying the tears she could no longer shed.

Because of the uncertainty of the weather, she'd decided not to say anything to the family when she left. She might not fly back right away. It would give her a little time to come to grips with what had happened.

Wherever Chris was, she was fairly certain he wasn't staying at home. Reporters would have staked out the place, waiting to talk to him about the situation. So she would stay at the house. Once she left his home, she would leave him the keys to the house and car he'd given her.

She slowed when she got to his driveway and noticed that he'd taken the name off his mailbox. No reason to advertise, she supposed, in case some enterprising soul hadn't as yet found him.

The place looked deserted. The grass needed trimming. The windows stared blankly, their draperies closed. She pulled around back and used the remote to open the garage door. There was no reason to advertise her presence, either.

Once inside, she looked around the kitchen. There were a couple of glasses sitting on the counter that hadn't been there when she left. So Chris had been here at one time.

She checked the refrigerator. She'd stocked it last week, thinking that she was setting up a routine for their marriage. Being back in the house was even more painful than she'd expected it to be. She'd hoped to be able to protect herself from hurt by holding on to her anger that Chris could so easily push her away, negating what they had together. Instead the pain seeped in when she remembered being here with him, his teasing her, his loving her.

Stop it! she admonished herself. *Haven't you already learned not to live in a fantasy world? The reality is that Chris doesn't want you.* There was no reason to think he ever did.

She went upstairs and when she reached the bedroom found the door shut. Opening it, she was surprised to find the room almost black. Drapes covered the windows. Chris must have come home to sleep during the day at one point, she decided.

She walked over and tugged on the draperies, opening them to the dreary light outside.

"Wha—? Who's there?" Chris's voice behind her caused her to jump in surprise. She spun around.

"Chris?"

From the light coming in through the window she saw him sprawled across the top of the bed, still dressed except for his shoes. His clothes were rumpled and he didn't look as though he'd shaved in a while.

"What are you doing here?" he asked, sitting up on the side of the bed and scrubbing his hand across his face.

"I was going to ask you the same thing."

He glanced up at her, his eyes bloodshot. "Well, hell, Maribeth. I live here. Where did you expect me to be?"

She was tempted to repeat his words back to him. Instead she said, "I thought you said you'd be working. Since you weren't answering your phone, I just thought—"

"I unplugged it days ago, not long after the story broke. Once the media found out the connection between me and my father, they wouldn't stop calling."

She walked over to the chest of drawers where she'd stored her things. Keeping her back to him, she asked, "Why didn't you return my calls that first night?"

He was quiet for a moment. Then he said, "It really doesn't matter at this point, does it?" He walked over to the bathroom and paused in the doorway. "You never said what you're doing here."

She turned and looked at him. He looked awful, as though he hadn't slept in days. Instead of answering him, she asked, "When was the last time you ate?"

"I don't remember."

"Why don't you get cleaned up and I'll have something ready for you to eat when you come down?"

"Why would you want to do anything for me? Didn't you hear anything I said last night?"

"Oh, yes. You said you'd like to hang on to the friendship. If that's all you want from me, I can accept that. I'm offering to feed you as a friend, not the woman you married."

For a moment she thought he'd flinched at the last word but when she continued to watch him, she decided she was mistaken. As usual, his expression gave nothing of his thoughts away.

She turned away and went downstairs, mentally running through what was there that she could quickly prepare for a hot meal.

Chris stood under the hard pressure of hot water beating down on him, wondering if he was ever going to wake up from the nightmare he'd found himself in.

When he'd first seen Maribeth standing there in the pale light from the window, he was certain he was hallucinating again. She'd been in his thoughts so much since the last time he'd seen her asleep in his bed that he assumed his mind had finally given way and conjured her here.

Why hadn't she had the sense to stay in Agua Verde where she belonged? She didn't deserve to be involved in this messy situation.

He'd once accused her of being naive. Hell, that was a laugh, wasn't it? Looking back, he could see that he'd been the one who'd been naive, blindly following orders, believing that he was working on the side of right and justice.

Wasn't he looking to stop the flow of drugs into the States? If he was assigned to work for his father, to follow his father's activities and report back, wasn't that part of it? Hadn't he felt self-righteous about what he was doing? If his father was doing something illegal, then he would be caught.

But what if his father wasn't doing something illegal? What if a few of his trusted executives had seen a way to make some money on the side and had carefully set it up to look as if it was the head of the company who was involved?

Chris was beginning to understand, much to his disgust at his own prejudices that had stopped him from seeing it sooner, how he had been used to help set up his father, to frame him. The first few days after the arrests had been made he'd begun to notice things he hadn't noticed before. He heard men he'd worked with deliberately lie about certain events that had taken place and he realized that he was in as deep trouble as his father.

All with a deliberate intent from someone within the agency.

He wasn't certain who was behind it, or how many agents had been in on the scheme. What he had to do was take responsibility for allowing himself to be used.

It was going to get much worse. He was going to be fighting a great many people on many different levels and issues. There was no way he could drag Maribeth into the mess. He had no guarantee that he would be able to prove anything. He refused to take her down with him.

She heard him on the stairs. By the time he reached the kitchen she had coffee and orange juice poured and was placing eggs, hash browns and bacon on a warmed plate.

"You look a little better," she observed judiciously. She nodded toward the table. "Eat."

"What about you?"

"I stopped a while ago and got something." She didn't want to admit that she hadn't been able to eat much since the last time she'd seen him. After their conversation last night, she could scarcely swallow anything.

Maribeth kept busy straightening the kitchen, wiping down the counters, anything so that she didn't have to look at Chris. The silence in the room seemed to develop its own weighty presence.

"Why did you come back, Maribeth?" he asked sometime later.

She glanced around and saw that he had eaten everything she'd put in front of him and was now drinking his third cup of coffee.

She sat down across from him and folded her hands on the table. "I could give you several reasons, all valid, but the truth of the matter is, I couldn't stay away. Those two weeks we were together may have meant nothing to you, Chris, but they changed my life in ways I'm only now beginning to understand. My home isn't in Agua Verde any longer. I can visit and I will because I love my sisters and their families but I can't go back there...not to live."

As though her answer would mean very little to him, he asked, "So what are you going to do?"

She looked away from him, staring sightlessly out the sliding glass door.

"I haven't gotten that far, yet. I wasn't here long enough to make any contacts. I'd had an idea of something I wanted to discuss with you the day Bobby showed up. I forgot to mention it then. And now? Well, I don't guess it would work for me."

"What was it?"

"I wanted to build a small horse barn back there—" she nodded toward the back of his property "—and maybe board or train horses, much like what I was doing with Travis, but on a much smaller scale."

"It wouldn't be a good idea to be anywhere around me at the moment. It's a good thing you haven't taken time to change your identification. The family name won't ever be quite so illustrious after all this."

"Do you think I care?"

"You should."

She studied him for a long time. "Is that why you said what you did last night? Are you under some misguided notion that you need to protect me from what has happened to your father?"

"It's not just that. I'm being pulled into it. No matter which way I go, I'm going to be made to look like I betrayed either the government investigation or my father."

"How?"

"It's complicated to explain and there's really no need. If you get out now, there's little damage done to your name or reputation."

"So you *are* trying to protect me! Just as you tried to protect me when Bobby got married. That's the reason you sent me back to Agua Verde, isn't it? Not because you were busy, but because of what was going to happen."

"I had no idea it was going to end up like this, believe me."

"Which gave you more reason to protect me. Chris, listen to me. I'm not a child any longer. Maybe it took me a while to grow up and understand how to be an adult, but that doesn't mean I'm not willing to take on the responsibility of being an adult."

"This isn't your fight."

"I know. But it's yours and you are my husband. Have you already forgotten those vows we took? Did you think they were just part of some meaningless ritual to go through? We committed our lives to each other, not just the good times or the fun times. We were fortunate to have those days for our honeymoon. It gave us a chance to forget about the world and discover each other, but we never pretended to each other that our life together would be spent in that way."

He gave her a lopsided smile. "I guess we did sort of blot out the world there for a while, despite everything going on around us."

"Without a doubt. And we can do it again, from time to time, but I expected to face some downtimes as well. I don't want to run from what's happening now. I want this marriage to work and I think it can, if you'll give it a chance.

"I know you don't love me, at least as you would a wife, but I know you care about me as a friend. Let me give you that friendship in return. You were there for me when I desperately needed someone. Will you let me be here for you now?"

They sat across the table from each other, each intently watching the other. Maribeth knew she was fighting for the life she wanted, if she could only break through the wall he kept around him.

"You don't think I love you?" he finally asked.

"Haven't you been listening to anything I've been saying?" she replied with frustration.

He leaned back in his chair and stared up at the ceiling. In a quiet, musing voice, he said, "I can't remember when I first realized that I loved you. I believe it was our junior year in high school when it finally occurred to me that what I felt for you was considerably more than friendship. But then, I always was a little slow where girls were concerned."

She straightened in her chair. What was he saying? "Chris?" she murmured.

"Up until then I just thought it was perfectly natural that I wanted to be around you all the time, that regardless of the mood I was in, being around you made me feel better. I never asked myself why I hated summers away or why I resented my father so much for taking me away from what I really wanted...which was to be with you."

She couldn't believe what she was hearing. "But you never said anything back then. Nothing."

He lowered his gaze to meet hers. "It would never have done any good. I always knew that. You've probably forgotten the times when you'd come to me upset because of something Bobby had said or done to hurt your feelings, but those were the times when it was the hardest for me not to betray what I was feeling to you."

She stared at him in wonder. "You always took up for him and made his behavior sound perfectly natural and ordinary, as though all boys acted that way."

He grinned. "Well, mostly that was true. We're not all that sensitive to a young girl's feelings."

"But you were."

He shook his head. "Not with everyone. Just to you. I could almost sense your mood or how you felt by the expression on your face. I can't tell you how many times

I just wanted to hold you in my arms and comfort you, instead of smoothing over whatever had happened."

The dull light was gradually fading but neither one of them turned on a lamp.

"So you weren't just doing me a favor by offering to marry me," she said softly.

"I thought I'd already made that clear."

"You love me." She felt the tension that she'd lived with for the past week dissolve within her.

"Yes."

She leaped up from her chair and lunged at him, almost knocking him out of his chair. "Then you're an even bigger idiot than I thought!" She shoved him away from the table, falling into his lap, and shook his shoulders. "How can you be so blind? Don't you know how much I love you and want to stay married to you? Can't you understand that you aren't the only one with deep feelings that go back into our shared past? I'll admit I was stupid not to understand that my feelings for Bobby were all mixed up with my feelings for our shared childhood and you and all that we had together. But it didn't take me long to figure out that what I was feeling for you had nothing to do with friendship."

He grinned at her ferocity and wrapped his arms around her. "Is this a proposal?"

She glared at him. "I don't have to propose to you, you big lug. I'm already married to you. I can't believe you can be so blind!"

"Maribeth?"

"What!"

"Kiss me."

That certainly took the wind out of her sails. "You're not going to send me away?"

"I should. It's the best thing I could do for you. But it took everything I could find inside me to force myself to tell you over the phone I didn't want to be married to you. There's no way in hell I can look you in the eye and say it."

She threw her arms around his neck and burst into tears. "Oh, Chris, I love you so much."

He stood, still holding her. "Before I have to go back to work, do you think you might be able to demonstrate some of that love for me?"

She kissed him and said, "I'll do my best, cowboy, I promise."

It was another five days before Chris could arrange to see his father. He'd had to pull in every favor he had with a lot of officials.

He no longer cared what visiting his father would look like. He didn't care about all the phrases being thrown around, such as "compromising the case against him," "hurting his image within the agency."

What he cared about was seeing his father again.

There were a few things he needed to tell him...things that he'd only come to understand since Maribeth had become a part of his life.

When his father was shown into the small room, Chris felt a lump form in his throat. He'd never seen his dad dressed in any way but the height of fashion. The orange coveralls were far from his usual attire.

There were lines on his face that hadn't been there before, but it was the pain in his eyes that hurt Chris the most.

"Thank you for seeing me," he said quietly once his father was seated. "I wouldn't have blamed you if you'd refused."

His father looked at him for a long moment, no doubt seeing the effect of the strain he'd been under, as well. "I've never refused you anything, son. Why would I start now?"

Chris almost lost his composure then. Why had he never seen that his father loved him? It had always been there. "I wanted to explain what I was doing working for you."

"You don't need to. I managed to figure that out on my own."

"I've worked for the agency since I first got out of school, Dad. It was something that I wanted to do, that I was good at."

"I wish I'd known. You have no idea how painful it was for me to see you taking those dead-end jobs rather than to work with me. If I'd ever needed proof of what you thought of me, that did it. But you were with the agency then, you say?"

"Yes." He took a deep breath and exhaled, trying to release some of the tension within him. "I have no excuse for my attitude toward you all these years, and no way to go back and undo what's been done between us. I couldn't see it, of course, not until Maribeth made me look at what I've been doing."

"How is she, by the way?"

"God, Dad, I don't know what I would do without her. I wake up at night sometimes afraid I dreamed it all and that she's actually married to someone else. The thing is, she's the one who made me look at how much I'm like you. We both want to be the one in control."

"I can't argue with you there."

"Neither of us seems to know how to compromise. I realize that I've been fighting you just for the sake of the fight. I used to accuse you and Mom of placing me in the middle of your power struggles. Only now I realize that I've been in a power struggle with you, myself."

"Well, I would say any power struggle we've been engaged in has been settled to your satisfaction. You've got me behind bars now."

"I don't believe you had anything to do with any of this," Chris said hoarsely.

"Oh? What makes you believe that?"

"I know you are determined to make it big in the business world. And you have. You did it all on your own, without anyone else's help."

"You could be describing yourself, you know."

"But you aren't greedy. You don't amass money for the sake of making money. The money part has always been the way you kept score...like Monopoly. You'd get no satisfaction in working to beat the system. You want to win using the system."

Kenneth studied him for several minutes without saying anything, then he nodded, a small smile hovering. "Yes, you definitely are my son. And you've reasoned it out without my help."

"I want you to know that I'm going to do everything I can to prove this case and to bring the real perps in. Right now they think they've got us just where they want us. With all the publicity you've been mentally convicted all over this country. I'm going to show them all they made a big mistake coming after a Cochran."

"Don't forget that I've got some good people in my corner, son. I always have. I don't care what it looks like,

I know I'm going to be able to prove that I wasn't involved."

"You've got to be worried, Dad. That's only natural."

"Not about me. I worry about Bambi. This has been tough on her. She hasn't had anyone to turn to that she can trust not to go to the tabloids with her concerns."

"Maribeth and I'll go over there this evening. It will do all three of us good to talk about it."

"You'd do that for me?"

"Isn't it about time I started acting like an adult where you're concerned?"

"Thank you, son. Just watch your back out there, and be careful who you trust."

"I've already figured that one out. I hope it isn't too late. They may end up throwing me in there with you, but somehow I don't think they'll push me that far. I happen to have a couple of friends who are helping me in the in-house investigation."

His dad smiled. "Go get 'em, tiger."

"We'll get Bambi to start planning the party we're going to have the day you walk out of here."

"Sounds good to me."

"I love you, Dad." It was the first time Chris had ever said it. He was amazed at how easy those words were to say to this man.

His dad blinked rapidly a few times and a muscle in his jaw clenched. Finally he nodded, saying, "The feeling's mutual, son. The feeling's mutual."

Epilogue

"**T**he press is having another field day," Maribeth commented, handing Chris the paper as soon as he walked into the kitchen. He leaned over and kissed her before sitting down to breakfast. "Mmm," she said dreamily, "you smell good."

"It's the after-shave."

"And you. What a combination."

"What's the paper say?"

"Oh, it's full of stories about the new information that was uncovered regarding the government's investigation of the money laundering. Everyone is pointing the finger at everyone else. They're talking about a shake-up at the agency, a full investigation, and so forth and so on. There's very little mention that the charges against your dad have been dropped and that he was released."

"No. That doesn't make the news. Only scandals and crooked agents."

"It's nice to know your name was cleared."

He grinned. "Yeah, I'll agree with that." He glanced at his watch. "When do you want to leave?"

"Sometime after breakfast. If we get down there by midafternoon, I'll be able to help Mollie in the kitchen. She says Thanksgiving is her favorite holiday at mealtime. Megan's been helping her this week, as well. She's doing fine, according to the doctor, but everyone hovers because of Deke."

He pulled her onto his lap and nuzzled her neck. "Are you going to tell them our news?"

"I thought I might wait until Christmas. I want to savor the secret for a while longer."

"Then you'd better muzzle Bambi. I think she's already bought out every baby department in the city, announcing to one and all that she's finally going to be a grandmother, as though she's been waiting for years."

They both laughed. "I'm glad they're going to Agua Verde with us. I want your dad to meet my family."

"Be prepared for him to insist that everyone come to his place for Christmas. You know how he can be. He'll have it all organized with a fleet of limos to bring them up here."

"Actually that might be fun. Wouldn't the kids love it? I think he's going to enjoy them, as well."

"So do I. I suppose I should have checked with you first before I told him about the baby."

"No, you did exactly what your heart told you to do. Never doubt a prompting from your heart. It's never wrong."

"Ah, Maribeth, you are something else. Have I told you how pleased I am to be married to you?"

"Not since you woke me up this morning." She gave him a lingering kiss, then smiled. "Can you think of a better Christmas gift in all the world than to know we've got a baby on the way?"

"What's just as important to me is that he or she is going to get to know his grandfather without any influence."

"You know your mother isn't going to like the changes you're making in your life."

"I know. But she'll have to deal with it. My grandfather reminded me that he's leaving the ranch to me. He already wants me to take more of an active role in the place."

"And you told him that you don't want any part of something that is controlled by the weather and market prices, right?"

"Actually I told him that we'd probably spend part of our time down there, even though I'll be spending much of my time working here with Dad."

"Maybe you can build a runway on the ranch, so we can fly back and forth."

"That's certainly a possibility." He set her on her feet and stood. "C'mon, let's get these dishes out of the way and finish packing. I'm eager to get on the road."

"You always look forward to returning to Agua Verde, don't you?"

"It was always the best part of my life. Or so I thought as a kid. I didn't realize it wasn't the place, it was you. I want to be wherever you are, making certain that you are happy."

"Funny. I feel the same way about you."

''That's probably why we've been friends for so many years. We have so much in common.''

He took her by the hand and they companionably went upstairs to find everything they intended to take to the families belonging to the O'Brien sisters of Agua Verde.

It was truly a time for thanksgiving.

*   *   *   *   *

COMING NEXT MONTH

It's Silhouette Desire's 1000th birthday! Join us for a spectacular three-month celebration, starring your favorite authors and the hottest heroes of the decade!

#997 BABY DREAMS—Raye Morgan
The Baby Shower
Sheriff Rafe Lonewolf couldn't believe his feisty new prisoner was the innocent woman she claimed to be. But a passionate night with Cami Bishop was suddenly making *him* feel criminal!

#998 THE UNWILLING BRIDE—Jennifer Greene
The Stanford Sisters
Paige Stanford's new neighbor was sexy, smart...and single! Little did she know Stefan Michaelovich wanted to make *her* his blushing bride!

#999 APACHE DREAM BRIDE—Joan Elliott Pickart
When Kathy Maxwell purchased a dream catcher, she had no idea she'd soon catch herself an Apache groom! But could her dream really come true...or would she have to give up the only man she ever loved?

#1000 MAN OF ICE—Diana Palmer
Silhouette Desire #1000!
After one tempestuous night with irresistible Barrie Bell, May's MAN OF THE MONTH, Dawson Rutherford, swore off love forever. Now the only way he could get the land he wanted was to make Barrie his temporary bride.

#1001 INSTANT HUSBAND—Judith McWilliams
The Wedding Night
Nick St. Hilarion needed a mother for his daughter, not a woman for himself to love! But when Ann Lennon arrived special delivery, he realized he might not be able to resist falling for his mail-order wife!

#1002 BABY BONUS—Amanda Kramer
Debut Author
Leigh Townsend was secretly crazy about sexy Nick Romano, but she wasn't going to push him to propose! So she didn't tell him he was going to be a daddy—or else he would insist on becoming a husband, too.

SILHOUETTE®

Desire®

CELEBRATION 1000

A treasured piece of romance could be yours!

During April, May and June as part of
Desire's Celebration 1000 you can enter to win an
original piece of art used on an actual Desire cover!

Or you could win one of 300 autographed Man of the
Month books!

See Official Sweepstakes Rules for more details.

To enter, complete an Official Entry Form or a 3"x5" card by hand printing
"Silhouette Desire Celebration 1000 Sweepstakes", your name and address, and
mail to: **In the U.S.:** Silhouette Desire Celebration 1000 Sweepstakes, P.O. Box
9069, Buffalo, N.Y. 14269-9069, or **In Canada:** Silhouette Desire Celebration 1000
Sweepstakes, P.O. Box 637, Fort Erie, Ontario L2A 5X3. Limit one entry per
envelope. Entries must be sent via first-class mail and be received no later than
6/30/96. No liability is assumed for lost, late or misdirected mail.

**Official Entry Form—Silhouette Desire Celebration 1000
Sweepstakes**

Name: _____

Address: _____

City: _____

State/Province: _____

Zip or Postal Code: _____

Favorite Desire Author: _____

Favorite Desire Book: _____

SWEEPS

SILHOUETTE DESIRE® "CELEBRATION 1000" SWEEPSTAKES
OFFICIAL RULES—NO PURCHASE NECESSARY

To enter, complete an Official Entry Form or a 3"x5" card by hand printing "Silhouette Desire Celebration 1000 Sweepstakes," your name and address, and mail it to: In the U.S.: Silhouette Desire Celebration 1000 Sweepstakes, P.O. Box 9069, Buffalo, NY 14269-9069, or in Canada: Silhouette Desire Celebration 1000 Sweepstakes, P.O. Box 637, Fort Erie, Ontario L2A 5X3. Limit one entry per envelope. Entries must be sent via first-class mail and be received no later than 6/30/96. No liability is assumed for lost, late or misdirected mail.

Prizes: Grand Prize—an original painting (approximate value $1500 U.S.);300 Runner-up Prizes—an autographed Silhouette Desire® Book (approximate value $3.50 U.S./$3.99 CAN. each). Winners will be selected in a random drawing (to be conducted no later than 9/30/96) from among all eligible entries received by D.L. Blair, Inc., an independent judging organization whose decision is final.

Sweepstakes offer is open only to residents of the U.S. (except Puerto Rico) and Canada who are 18 years of age or older, except employees and immediate family members of Harlequin Enterprises Ltd., their affiliates, subsidiaries, and all agencies, entities and persons connected with the use, marketing or conduct of this sweepstakes. All federal, state, provincial, municipal and local laws apply. Offer void where prohibited by law. Taxes and/or duties are the sole responsibility of the winners. Any litigation within the province of Quebec respecting the conduct and awarding of prizes may be submitted to the Regle des alcools des courses et des jeux. All prizes will be awarded; winners will be notified by mail. No substitution for prizes is permitted. Odds of winning are dependent upon the number of eligible entries received.

Grand Prize winner must sign and return an Affidavit of Eligibility within 30 days of notification. In the event of noncompliance within this time period, prize may be awarded to an alternate winner. Any prize or prize notification returned as undeliverable may result in the awarding of that prize to an alternate winner. By acceptance of their prize, winners consent to the use of their names, photographs or likenesses for purposes of advertising, trade and promotion on behalf of Harlequin Enterprises Ltd., without further compensation unless prohibited by law. In order to win a prize, residents of Canada will be required to correctly answer a time-limited arithmetical skill-testing question administered by mail.

For a list of winners (available after October 31, 1996) send a separate self-addressed stamped envelope to: Silhouette Desire Celebration 1000 Sweepstakes Winners, P.O. Box 4200, Blair, NE 68009-4200.

SWEEPR

As seen on TV!
Free Gift Offer

With a Free Gift proof-of-purchase from any Silhouette® book, you can receive a beautiful cubic zirconia pendant.

This gorgeous marquise-shaped stone is a genuine cubic zirconia—accented by an 18" gold tone necklace.

(Approximate retail value $19.95)

Send for yours today...
compliments of ▼ *Silhouette*®

To receive your free gift, a cubic zirconia pendant, send us one original proof-of-purchase, photocopies not accepted, from the back of any Silhouette Romance™, Silhouette Desire®, Silhouette Special Edition®, Silhouette Intimate Moments® or Silhouette Shadows™ title available in February, March or April at your favorite retail outlet, together with the Free Gift Certificate, plus a check or money order for $1.75 U.S./$2.25 CAN. (do not send cash) to cover postage and handling, payable to Silhouette Free Gift Offer. We will send you the specified gift. Allow 6 to 8 weeks for delivery. Offer good until April 30, 1996 or while quantities last. Offer valid in the U.S. and Canada only.

Free Gift Certificate

Name: _____

Address: _____

City: _____ State/Province: _____ Zip/Postal Code: _____

Mail this certificate, one proof-of-purchase and a check or money order for postage and handling to: SILHOUETTE FREE GIFT OFFER 1996. In the U.S.: 3010 Walden Avenue, P.O. Box 9057, Buffalo NY 14269-9057. In Canada: P.O. Box 622, Fort Erie,

---

FREE GIFT OFFER
ONE PROOF-OF-PURCHASE

079-KBZ-R

To collect your fabulous FREE GIFT, a cubic zirconia pendant, you must include this original proof-of-purchase for each gift with the properly completed Free Gift Certificate.

079-KBZ-R

You're About to Become a *Privileged Woman*

Reap the rewards of fabulous free gifts and benefits with proofs-of-purchase from Silhouette and Harlequin books

Pages & Privileges™

It's our way of thanking you for buying our books at your favorite retail stores.

PROOF OF PURCHASE

SD-PP123

Offer expires October 31, 1996

**Harlequin and Silhouette—
the most privileged readers in the world!**

For more information about Harlequin and Silhouette's PAGES & PRIVILEGES program call the Pages & Privileges Benefits Desk: 1-503-794-2499

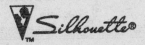

Silhouette®

SD-PP123